Brian let his hands roam.

Up and down Piper's back, drawing her more fully against him. She tore her mouth from his and her head dropped back as she took in a deep breath.

He drew one finger down the center of her sternum, tracing the circular gold charm that was nestled right above her cleavage before moving his hand farther down. Tracing the side of her breasts and feeling her heartbeat race as he did so.

He lowered his mouth again, wanting to kiss her slowly. Wanting to take his time and make this moment last. Needing her more than he needed his next breath, he knew that going slow would be impossible.

He needed to claim her as his.

* * *

In Bed with His Rival
by Katherine Garbera is part of the
Texas Cattleman's Club: Rags to Riches series.

Dear Readers,

As I write this, we are in the midst of lockdown. I hope by the time this book is in your hands that it is a distant memory and that your families and friends are all well and safe.

I love to write books set in Texas because Texas is in my heart. This book is set in Dallas and in the fictional town of Royal, but I lived in a North Dallas suburb for five years.

I loved Piper from the moment that she stepped on the page. She's a woman who spoke to me on so many levels. I loved that I was able to incorporate my own love of art and the art world into her character. As I was writing the book, Keanu Reeves's girlfriend, Alexandra Grant, was in the news and I used her for inspiration!

Brian was a lot of fun, as well. He's a total Texas man. He loves his family, football and has a strong work ethic that defines who he is. He's also a man who's not afraid to go after what or who he wants. Rivalries and family dynamics won't stop him from getting Piper.

The Texas Cattleman's Club series books are always fun to write because I get to be a part of the larger writing community. Talking and communicating with the other authors is one of the best parts.

Happy reading,

Katherine

KATHERINE GARBERA

IN BED WITH HIS RIVAL

Special thanks and acknowledgment are given
to Katherine Garbera for her contribution to the
Texas Cattleman's Club: Rags to Riches miniseries.

HARLEQUIN®
DESIRE™

Recycling programs
for this product may
not exist in your area.

ISBN-13: 978-1-335-20944-3

In Bed with His Rival

Harlequin Enterprises ULC
22 Adelaide St. West, 40th Floor
Toronto, Ontario M5H 4E3, Canada
www.Harlequin.com

Printed in U.S.A.

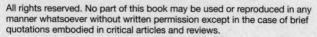

Katherine Garbera is the *USA TODAY* bestselling author of more than ninety-five books. Her writing is known for its emotional punch and sizzling sensuality. She lives in the Midlands of the UK with the love of her life; her son, who recently graduated university; and a spoiled miniature dachshund. You can find her online at www.katherinegarbera.com and on Facebook, Twitter and Instagram.

Books by Katherine Garbera

Harlequin Desire

The Wild Caruthers Bachelors

Tycoon Cowboy's Baby Surprise
The Tycoon's Fiancée Deal
Craving His Best Friend's Ex

One Night

One Night with His Ex
One Night, Two Secrets
One Night to Risk It All
Her One Night Proposal

Visit her Author Profile page at Harlequin.com,
or katherinegarbera.com, for more titles.

You can also find Katherine Garbera on Facebook,
along with other Harlequin Desire authors,
at Facebook.com/harlequindesireauthors.

Shout-out to Texas ladies!
Penni Askew, who welcomed me to Texas
when I moved there so long ago.
Kim Gammill and Kathy Ranney,
who were my mom buddies and friends
when I needed one. Eve Gaddy,
who is my soul sister.

One

Piper Holloway loved a wedding. Who didn't? They were joyous events.

Her niece Harley and Grant Everett had waited a long time for their happily ever after. Piper didn't begrudge them their wedded bliss, but a part of her wished she wasn't going stag to all of their festivities.

These happy-couple kind of events always made her reevaluate her life choices, even though she was perfectly content as a single woman. She had her art, which was way more reliable than a man, and a thriving—well *previously* thriving—business. Though she had never had any stake in Wingate Enterprises, many people suspected she might be part of its allegedly shady business dealings, and her clientele was down recently.

But none of that mattered. She was here to celebrate her niece's wedding day and support her sister, Ava, who'd recently gone through a really tough decision to move out of Keith's house and set up her own residence. Standing on her own after the death of her husband had been a struggle for Ava and she'd leaned on her good friend Keith until she'd realized he wanted a romantic relationship with her. Now, they all needed a fun day.

It was a gorgeous November Saturday in Royal, Texas. As much as Piper loved living in Dallas, there were times when she truly missed Royal, though she had been home a lot recently as her sister and family navigated their way through their business scandal. Of course, she didn't miss the gossips who'd been making her family's life a living hell since the drug-trafficking scandal had broken.

All of the Wingate assets had been frozen and their home seized. Harley wasn't able to be married on the Wingate estate, which Piper knew had been a dream of hers. But Grant's family's ranch was perfect for the small wedding celebration. It was mainly family and friends—those who had stuck by the Wingates and Holloways through thick and thin.

The Everett ranch was large and sprawling, and the grounds were decked out for the wedding, which had been beautiful. Harley was big into the environment and her choice of venue reflected that. Therefore, it seemed apt that she and Grant had decided to be married in the old barn, which had been decorated under the supervision of her older sister, Beth. The chairs were lined up, and despite the fact that the Wingates were no longer the favored family in Royal, there was a nice intimate group of attendees.

Everyone was happy that "Uncle" Keith wasn't in attendance today, mainly because of how that would have affected Ava. Piper's sister was still dealing with the heartbreak of losing her beloved husband a little over a two years ago and no one had approved of Keith's interest in her. Piper had kept her mouth shut because she didn't like to fight with Ava, especially over men, but it had seemed to her that Keith had been a little too overprotective of Ava. Her spunky sister had become a shell of the woman she had once been.

Right now Ava looked gorgeous in her mother-of-the-bride dress, but she seemed tired and thinly drawn. Moving out of Keith's house had only been the first step to Ava taking back her own life. Piper thought that Ava was finally getting past the crippling grief. Though Piper would never say it to her, the events of the last few months had certainly taken a toll on the Wingate matriarch. Ava was nineteen years older, and Piper had always craved her sister's attention and approval.

"What's that you're wearing?" Ava asked, coming

up behind her. "Even though the wedding is small, you could have made more of an effort."

Piper turned to face her sister, biting her tongue as she always did. Ava was in a mood and Piper was giving her a little leeway, given that she'd lost her home, her husband and was on the verge of losing her company, as well.

"It's a designer Grecian gown," Piper said, air kissing her sister's cheeks. "I thought it would be perfect for this occasion and when I texted Harley, she said it was fine. Have you heard any news on the investigation?"

"No. I believe Miles is getting closer but there is still nothing but rumors," Ava replied.

"Do they have any suspects?" Piper asked. She wasn't too close to the business side of things, but she knew that Ava was trying to get back into running the company so she would have something to do. But now, with the precarious state of affairs, those plans were up in the air.

"Yes, but I can't really share that with you," Ava told her in a terse tone. "I know you've never been married, but this really isn't the kind of conversation anyone wants to overhear on their wedding day."

"Of course, Ava. I see Zeke and Reagan waving me over. I'll catch up with you later. I'm sure you need to circulate as the mother of the bride, especially since Trent is not here."

Trent Wingate's death had left a hole in all of their

lives, and Piper knew that Harley missed her beloved father terribly. She'd escaped to Thailand to start her own business, which was thriving now.

Piper knew her words hadn't been nice, but her sister had a way of making her react like a…bitch. She turned, thinking she should apologize, but Ava had already moved away. There were times when she wondered if anyone could melt the ice around her sister's heart. Piper didn't want to impose on her nephew and his new wife, so she drifted toward the bar.

"Buy you a drink?" a man asked. His voice was dark, sexy and straight out of dreams that she channeled into her art.

She turned to see Brian Cooper standing behind her. He was tall, over six feet, and had thick, close-cut black hair that made his face seem all strong, masculine angles. He had an easy smile and his eyes beamed with intelligence. He'd asked her to coffee more than once and she'd always said no.

He ticked a lot of her boxes. Whip smart with oodles of charisma…and the innate ability to make her forget things that she shouldn't. She really believed in the adage *older and wiser*. Which was why she had decided to stay away from him.

But it wasn't just the age difference—she was nearly eleven years older—but also the fact that he was Keith Cooper's nephew. Keith had gone from being a family friend to Ava's overprotective friend, and that complicated things. Piper preferred to keep things simple. It just was easier.

"It's an open bar," she pointed out.

He waggled his eyebrows at her. "I know. Figured this way you wouldn't say no."

He was effortlessly charming with the kind of square jaw and impish grin that made her pulse beat a little bit faster. She'd tried to be subtle when she turned him down, but as she'd already observed, Brian was a very smart man. "I'd love tequila straight. But Ava would have a fit if I had one, so sauvignon blanc please."

"Do you always do what Ava wants?" he asked. "She has so much power over everyone in her circle."

"Even your uncle," she pointed out. Keith had been rumored to be taking Ava's decision to distance herself from him without grace.

"Yeah, I guess. I don't really see that much of him normally. I have been busy opening my own law firm in Dallas," he said, then he groaned. "Did I really just say that out loud?"

She had to laugh at the way he said it. "Yes, you did."

"I wasn't bragging. I was just trying—"

"It's okay. What do you want to drink?" she asked as they moved forward and were next in line at the bar.

"Grey Goose on the rocks," he said.

"Damn. Now I'm beginning to rethink my promise to be classy and have white wine," she lamented.

"Why not just be yourself and have what you want?" he asked. "But then again, I'm not related to Ava Wingate..."

Piper appreciated Brian's acknowledgement of that, and yet at the same time, he reminded her that it had been far too long since she'd just let go and been herself. That thought was at the top of her mind as she stepped forward and ordered their drinks, getting the tequila for herself.

She turned to Brian and handed him his glass as they walked away from the bar toward the side of the dance floor. The band was playing and couples moved to the music, but they stood far enough away that they could still hear each other.

"I think I am a bad influence," Brian remarked. "But I don't regret it. Cheers."

"Cheers," Piper said, clinking her glass to his. Although she didn't comment on his admission, she had to admit the tequila tasted *way* better than a glass of wine would have. And truth be told? She felt like herself instead of the perfect sister she tried to be every time she arrived back in Royal. Piper hated that she was forty and still trying to get Ava's approval.

"You just reminded me it's okay to have fun," she said. "I am a little disappointed that I needed that, but I'm glad you did."

* * *

Brian enjoyed the vodka but sipped it slowly. It seemed like forever, but in reality, it had only been a few months since he'd first noticed Piper Holloway. She had a cool, funky aura and of course she was so damned hot. He wanted her. She plagued his dreams and left him waking up with a hard-on, and if he was being honest, he'd thought he was way past those days.

He'd asked other women out and taken them home, but no one could satisfy that Piper-sized ache in his gut. He was pretty sure it was just lust and the more she turned him down, the more determined he was to have her.

Possibly he was wrong and the sizzle between them would fade out after they had a drink. His intuition said that would never happen and it rarely steered him wrong. But Piper had been pretty hard to reel in, no matter what he tried.

Was it pride?

He hoped it was something more than that, but as he stood next to her sipping vodka and finally having the conversation he wanted, he didn't care.

They really didn't have much in common—after all, she was a free-spirited artist and he was a high-powered family law attorney—but there was something to be said about opposites attracting...

His eyes slowly drifted over her again.

Piper had a creative vibe, from the way she wore

her hair—this month colored dark brown—in an angled bob that was longer in the front than the back, to her Grecian-styled gown in a vibrant sapphire color with a plunging neckline that revealed the inner curves of her luscious breasts.

She was tall, at least five-seven, but she wore heels, giving herself another couple of inches and making it so they came eye to eye. He watched as she savored the tequila, closing her eyes when she took a sip. There was something wildly erotic about the way she drank it, and he knew he needed to play it cool, but he couldn't help but think of throwing back shots with her alone in his place.

God, he could picture her standing next to him in nothing. Hell…just the thought made him rock hard. Earthy and sensual, a bona fide modern goddess, and even though his family and hers had grown apart, he couldn't care less.

"I stopped by your gallery a few weeks ago but you weren't there," Brian said, realizing he needed to up his game around this woman. First, he'd sounded like a braggart talking about his law firm and now this clumsy conversational gambit.

"I was out of town," she replied. "I didn't know you were coming by."

"Of course… I guess I should have called first."

"That's always a good idea," she said.

"But you haven't always been receptive to meeting me," he reminded her. "I did ask you out for coffee at Zeke's."

She flushed and tipped her head to the side. "To be honest, I wasn't sure of you. I don't really like the influence Keith had over my sister after Trent's death. I wasn't sure you weren't the same kind of man."

That was a blow, but not unexpected. She was cautious and he guessed he didn't blame her. While their families weren't the Capulets and the Montagues, they also weren't close as they'd once been, before Trent's death. Brian's friendship with Zeke had made him aware that Ava's family wasn't overly fond of his uncle. And in all honesty, he had thought it a little unseemly how quickly Keith had moved in on Ava after Trent's death. But Ava had seemed to need someone to lean on.

"Fair enough. I'm not my uncle, but I can understand where you are coming from," he said.

"Thanks," she said dryly.

He groaned and realized he either needed more vodka or just to stop talking. The music changed to one of those group dances, the Electric Slide, and Piper looked over at him. "I love this song. Want to dance?"

"I can't dance," he confessed.

"Catch you later then," she said, handing him her empty tequila glass and making her way out onto the dance floor. He stood there, watching her move. There was a smile on her face that lit up the entire room. She moved with lithe, graceful steps, holding the hand of her great-nephew, Daniel, and showing him the moves.

"Dude, why are you standing here instead of dancing with the woman you've been trying to get with for months?" Zeke asked him.

"I can't dance," he repeated to his friend. "It's a disaster and I pretty much haven't been very articulate with Piper tonight, so I don't think I need another strike against me."

His friend just shook his head. "The Electric Slide isn't my thing either, but if your lady wants to be on the dance floor, then that's where you should be."

"She's not my lady," Brian grumbled.

"She never will be if you stand here like a doofus," Zeke pointed out. He left to find Reagan, and a few minutes later Brian saw the two of them dancing along with everyone else.

Brian had never let anything stand in the way of what he wanted and he certainly wasn't about to be defeated by this dance. He finished his vodka in one long swallow, put the empty glasses on the tray of a passing waiter and went for it.

He joined the group on the dance floor next to Daniel. "Hey, can you help me figure this out?"

"Sure can," the four-year-old said. Then Daniel started calling out the steps, and to Brian's surprise, it was actually fun.

Piper looked over at him, laughing when he and

Daniel went the wrong way and almost crashed into the line behind them. Finally, the music ended, and Brian stooped down to thank Daniel. The little boy was very happy that he had a starring role in the day's events as his parents had been married. He looked adorable in his tux, cowboy boots and Stetson.

"You really helped me out. I owe you, buddy," Brian said.

"I like jelly beans," Daniel returned with a grin.

"I'll remember that." The music changed to a slower song, and Brian looked over at Piper. "Dance with me?"

"I'd say no, but you really put yourself out there with the Slide," she said, taking his hand and coming into his arms.

A tingle went through him, and his blood seemed to run heavier in his veins. More than anything, he wanted to take her back to his place here in Royal, but that felt like it might be too fast for this woman who he'd barely been able to get to have a drink with him. Was he coming on too strong? Hell, he didn't know another way to be when he wanted something.

And he definitely wanted Piper in his bed.

But if he'd learned anything from this woman today, it was that she was skittish.

Building trust took time, and Brian had never been long on patience, but for Piper he was willing to be. He wanted to explore his attraction for her and wouldn't let anything stand in his way.

And the attraction that burned between the two of them might be setting him on fire but he wanted to stoke the flames, not just let it go wild and leave nothing but ashes and smoke.

Piper wanted to pretend that she wasn't interested in Brian Cooper, but after spending some time on the dance floor in his arms she knew that was a lie. The large tent that had been erected in the yard of the Everett ranch had sparkling lights draped around the interior and large portable heaters dotted around the area to keep the November chill away. The reception was full of people she'd known her entire life, but after the scandal that her family had been through lately, Piper realized these were the people who mattered. The ones who'd stood by the Wingates and hadn't abandoned them.

Brian was one of those men. He'd helped Zeke and Reagan out—her nephew had told her how much it had meant to them. And, of course, there was this crazy sexual attraction between her and Brian. It had been there since the moment they'd met but she'd done her best to ignore it. That kind of passion she reserved for her art. It was safer that way. She just had never been an all-or-nothing kind of woman when it came to her desires, and with Brian it felt dangerous to let go.

Though with his hand on her back and her breasts brushing his chest as they danced, she was sorely tempted to throw caution to the wind. There was something...*electric*...in the way he touched her, and despite what he'd said about not dancing, he wasn't half bad, swaying to the beat.

She started to feel restless. Usually she didn't feel it in Dallas because she had her routines and her normal life. But here in Royal, when everything was in chaos with her family, it felt like things were changing... Maybe she was too. Starting with when she had ordered that tequila. She'd spent too long trying to be part of the society that Ava always urged her to conform to. Now she was on the edge, ready to do something reckless...

But, as attracted as she was to him, she knew that Brian wasn't the man for her.

He was a family friend. More so than "Uncle" Keith, who Piper's nieces and nephews didn't trust after the way he'd muscled his way into Ava's life after the death of their father. Should she be equally careful of Brian...?

"Another drink?" he asked when the song ended.

"That'd be great," she said.

"Piper, do you have a minute?" Lauren Roberts asked, coming over to her.

"Go on. I'll get our drinks and come find you," Brian said. He turned to walk away, and she watched him go, admiring the cut of his suit.

Down, girl.

"What can I help you with?" Piper asked, pivoting toward Lauren. The brunette beauty was known around Royal for her fabulous food trucks, and her assistant had mentioned Lauren was going to be opening a restaurant soon.

"I was in your gallery while you were out of town and saw a number of pieces I really liked. Your assistant said that it would be better to talk to you so that you'd have a feel for what I really wanted," Lauren said. "I know a wedding reception isn't the ideal place to chat, but I was hoping to catch you so I wouldn't have to go back to Dallas next week. Do you mind?"

Piper shook her head. "No, of course not. I love talking about art, and finding pieces that suit your new restaurant sounds like a fun project. I think someone had mentioned it was going to be a farm-to-table one?"

"Yes. I really want to be as local as I can with the sourcing of the food," the other woman said.

"I think the art should be from the area too," Piper mused, thinking out loud. "I have a few colleagues that I can reach out to in order to find some local artists. Are you looking for paintings or photography?"

"I just want really good stuff on the walls so people will feel like they are in a nice place," Lauren said.

Piper laughed. "So, you're saying you'll know what you want when you see it?"

"Yes. Also Gracie Diaz is investing in my business so she'll be helping me make the choices."

"Okay, let me look around and see what I can find. I'll send some images to the two of you and you can narrow down what you like. Then we can go forward from there. How does that sound?" Piper asked.

"Perfect. Thank you," Lauren said. "I know it's not my business…but are you seeing Brian?"

"No. We're just hanging out together. I guess he didn't bring a date either," Piper said.

"That's good," Lauren said. "I'm sure he's not anything like Keith. I know Sutton thinks he seems like a good guy."

Seemed like a good guy.

"Great," Piper said.

"What's great?" Brian asked, handing her a glass of tequila as Lauren turned to leave.

"The reception," Lauren said, walking away.

"It is nice," Brian told Piper. "I really like that Harley and Grant found each other and that they are going to go back to Thailand. There was a time when everyone would have expected her to give up her life and move back here."

"Not that long ago," Piper said. "Grant's a great guy. I think that even though times have changed, some men still wouldn't follow their woman."

Brian took a sip of his vodka and rubbed the back

of his neck. "I'm not sure I'd leave the country, but I who am I to judge someone else?"

"Right. Everyone makes the choices that work for them," Piper concurred.

Watching her niece, she was happy for Harley but another part of her was…leery. Piper had once come close to believing she'd found someone she could share her life with, but she hadn't measured up to his version of perfection and he'd left. And although it had stung for a time, life hadn't ended. She was old enough to know she didn't need a man by her side to complete her. But spending the reception with Brian…exploring the spark of sensuality he'd lit in her…had shown her that she had missed the companionship of having a partner. Not that Brian would be her partner, but maybe it was time for her to start looking again.

She had been put off dating after her bad breakup and watching Ava's marriage to Trent as his health deteriorated. But her nieces and nephews were all finding love and that made her long for something to help fill the void.

That said, she would never try to change for a man again. And she'd never be with a guy she couldn't trust. But laughing and talking with Brian had reminded her of how much she'd shut herself off from relationships. Maybe it was fear or something else that had kept her away, but it was time to stop it.

She turned her attention to the coming week. She

was looking forward to getting back to Dallas. Even though he had a law firm in the big D, he wasn't part of her circle. Once she was home, she'd be away from the confusion and desire that Brian was stirring in her.

Two

The Dallas art district was downtown in the city's cultural hub. The strikingly angular Meyerson Symphony Center and the lavish Winspear Opera House gave the area its grounding. Piper's gallery was close to the Nasher Sculpture Center with its exhibits of modern masterpieces in a verdant setting. She had worked hard to be able to have her gallery in the art district instead of on the outskirts of town, but it was important for her clients to know that she was a respectable art dealer. Today she'd started her morning walking through the Crow Collection of Asian Art displays. Sometimes she needed to recharge her inner artist. Especially now.

Wednesdays had traditionally been when she did her accounting and read the reports her accountant sent over. But since the trouble with the Wingate company started and the scandal had broken there had been a steady decline in profits. And if the black-and-white numbers in front of her weren't enough evidence, she also had realized that the gallery crowds were thinner. She could blame the economy, but the truth was no one wanted to be associated with someone—even on the fringes—who'd had assets seized by the DEA.

She'd had one client even go so far as to ask if she could provide proof of her due diligence on the provenance for a painting that they'd purchased almost five years ago. She'd done it, but it had ticked her off because she had never taken a penny of Wingate money and she'd always run her gallery with a strong moral and ethical code. But she couldn't fight whispers, and if she was going to be painted with the same brush as her sister and nieces and nephews, she was going to have to look at a way to expand her business. Find a new revenue stream.

"Hey, boss, here's your chai latte," Coco said, coming in and dropping it on her desk. "Also, Gracie Diaz called a few minutes ago and asked if you had time to see her this afternoon."

"Thanks for the latte," Piper said. "I believe my afternoon is open. I already pulled some slides.

Would you mind assembling them in viewing room A?"

"Not at all. And I'll arrange a time with Gracie and put it on your calendar. Also, we've had a few requests for commission work. I know you have the gala piece going up next week. Are you interested?"

"Probably," Piper said. "You know how busy the holiday season can be. We need to also see about renting out the space at night for office parties like we did last year."

Coco sat down in the guest chair and propped her combat-booted feet on the corner of Piper's desk. "I've already started. I have three parties lined up so far and I've got two more who should get back to me next week. One client wondered if we could hang something modern, similar to the party in that *Love Actually* movie. I told them we'd see. We do have those nudes from Maxi that seemed like they might work."

"I like that idea. I'll go over to the warehouse later this week and see what we have. Put on your event planner hat and see if we can do something more with this concept. We need to make a push through the holidays to drive revenue."

"No problem, boss," Coco said.

One of her other assistants—Paul—came to her door. "There's a Brian Cooper here to see you."

"He's been here before," Coco murmured. "Kind

of cute, easy smile, nice ass. Want me to talk to him for you?"

"I've got it. Get to work on those paintings for Gracie and get that firmed up. Paul, Coco's going to need your help with a themed office party," Piper said, leaving her assistants and heading out onto the balcony where all of the offices were.

She looked down onto the main gallery floor where Brian was easy to spot. He stood in front of a kinetic wire sculpture she'd collaborated with a local spoken-word poet to create. It was called *The Border* and spoke directly about Xavier's struggle to stay on the right side of the law. The sculpture was one body but two faces looking in different directions. One contemplative, the other angry. In one hand was a notepad and pen, in the other, a gun. She was proud of it but she saw the parts she could still improve. For instance, the angle of the jaw on one side was sharper than the other.

As much as she loved creating, there was also a part of her that hated it. Seeing the image in her head and then witnessing how close she got to it, without ever quite reaching it, was a constant struggle.

She tucked a strand of hair behind her ear and shook off that mood as she approached Brian. He wore a suit that was cut to fit his broad shoulders and tapered to his narrow waist sending a sensual thrill through her.

"Hello, Brian. I wasn't expecting to see you today," she said,

He turned to face her with a good-natured smile, drawing her gaze to his mouth. He had full, chiseled lips that looked like they were made for kissing. She should have kissed him on Saturday at the reception so she'd have that out of the way. Instead she was staring and wondering how his firm mouth would feel pressed against hers.

"I hope you don't mind. I was in the area for a client meeting and thought I'd stop in and see if you had time for lunch?"

"Um," she said, thrown. He had mentioned seeing her and she'd had time to think about it since the wedding. She'd decided to stop running from him. "Let me check my schedule. I told my assistant I was free for an appointment this afternoon. I'm helping Gracie Diaz pick out some art for Lauren's new restaurant."

"Sure. I'll wait while you check," he said. "I can't believe she won the lottery. I've never known anyone who won before."

"Me either," Piper replied as she scrolled through her calendar. A part of her hoped she had a lunchtime meeting scheduled, but then realized how cowardly that was.

Even though, in her defense, she knew she was just being cautious.

Brian raised all kinds of emotional red flags for

her. He was a man who knew what he wanted and wasn't afraid to go after it. That appealed to her on so many levels. Which was beyond dangerous.

Especially now, when he was watching her with an intensity she'd have to be blind to ignore.

She opened the group chat app her staff used so she could let Coco know she was going to go out for lunch with Brian. "Looks like I'm all yours."

"Great!" he said.

"What'd you have in mind?"

"Well, this is your neighborhood. Do you have a place you like to go?" he asked.

Piper had to smile at the way he didn't seem to mind putting the ball in her court. She realized this was a small thing, but she knew his uncle would never have let Ava pick a place.

There was more to Brian than what she'd come to know of the Cooper family. Or was she simply seeing that to justify her attraction to him?

"There is a really great street taco place around the corner. It's casual, pretty much outdoor seating."

"It's a nice day," he said. "I'm game for whatever you suggest."

"That's exactly what I like to hear," she murmured, dropping her phone into one of the pockets of her duster cardigan. He might be the one pursuing her, but she *wasn't* his prey, and deep down she wanted him too. Maybe enough to take him to her bed? She wasn't sure yet, but she wasn't ruling it out. It had been too long since she'd simply let herself go.

Brian followed Piper, watching the sway of her hips and the way that each step she took seemed to be designed to turn him on. When he'd driven by her shop he'd decided to build on the ground work he'd laid on Saturday at the wedding. He wasn't going to let her shove him back into the acquaintance zone. Brian had had too many long, restless nights of dreaming about her and knew that the time to try to exorcise her from his mind with other women had passed.

He needed Piper. Naked and willing and *his*.

However, he had the feeling that if he pushed too hard, she'd write him off and walk away. So he'd stacked the deck in his favor, making sure he had the right suit on today. One that showed off his success without saying he was trying too hard.

She led the way up the block and stopped shading her eyes against the sun. "Did you just happen by or was this planned?"

"Happened by," he said. Just because he was craving her as much as his next breath didn't mean she had to know. He had seen how badly damaged his uncle was when Ava had moved out of his place without taking his feelings into account. It had seemed… callous. And he wasn't sure that Piper wasn't the same way. Maybe she got off on teasing a man and watching him fall for her.

After all, she was single by choice.

"Oh." She sounded disappointed.

"Also I just opened a big office building and I'm in desperate need for someone with a good eye to help me pick the art for the lobby and the walls. I want to incorporate Texas art but also relevant modern stuff."

She tipped her head to the side. "I haven't done a lot of that type of work, but I do like the sound of it. Since this is a business lunch, I should take you somewhere nicer than—"

"Don't be silly. I'd rather eat at your favorite place while we talk than anywhere else," he said.

The November day was sunny and bright, and as they walked through the art district in downtown Dallas, he couldn't help but notice how Piper fit in with this neighborhood. While at the wedding, she'd stood out. She'd been an exotic flower among the Texas roses that were her nieces and her older sister, but here she made sense.

Brian realized that he, however, didn't fit in. He looked and felt too corporate. Not really a part of this world, but he admitted to himself that that was the appeal of Piper. She knew her own mind and was her own woman. A lot of the gals he'd dated lately had been looking to him to help shape who they were.

She wasn't like the other women he encountered. That was part of why he'd initially been drawn to her.

Dancing with her on Saturday, talking to her at the reception, had just honed that desire from lust at first sight into something more tangible. She wasn't just an attractive woman to him, she was *more*. And working with her on his building would be the first step to seeing how much more to him she would be. This spark between them would most likely never develop into anything more than a few nights together, but he was willing to take that chance. He needed to get this lust under control and return to his real life.

"Okay then. Do you want only established artists?" she asked once they'd ordered their food and were sitting at small table set apart from the others to the side of the food truck.

Brian finished chewing the bite he'd taken then wiped his hands. He hadn't given the project much thought beyond his initial conception. "I want the place to give anyone who comes in the feeling that they are going to be successful. If you recommend an artist who you think is a good investment then I trust your judgment."

"I'll need to see the space," she said. "Do you have any artists that you really like?"

"I can send you a list if you want. I have some ideas of what I don't like. We specialize in family law so I don't want anything too abstract. It should convey a sense of stability and unity. Even though legally their world is changing, we want them to feel secure."

She smiled at him. "I've never heard a lawyer talk like that."

He shrugged. "I'm not like other lawyers."

"I'm getting that. When did you come back to Dallas?"

"Sunday morning. You?" he asked.

"Sunday evening. I stayed with Ava and caught up with her," Piper said.

"How is it, having your sister so much older?" he asked.

"I don't know anything else, so it seems normal to me. Of course, my nieces and nephews are all more my contemporaries than Ava is, but it's just how our relationship has always been."

"That makes sense. When I was younger, I used to wish for siblings but I don't know that I would have liked it. I'm pretty competitive with just me. If you add others to the mix…"

"Disaster?"

"Maybe. I don't know," he said wryly. "I can't imagine being any other way."

"Me either," Piper admitted. "It has caused some friction with Ava over the years. She wants me to be more like…everyone else, I guess. She grew up with such a firm vision of the perfect family she wanted to create, and anything that doesn't match that image is a problem for her."

"You were a problem?"

"I tried not to be, but I can't conform to what anyone else wants me to be," she said.

And that was why he was sitting across from her on this Wednesday afternoon getting wildly aroused while they discussed business. But there was a part of him that felt like this was more than just lust. And yet another part of him didn't trust what was happening between them because she was Ava's sister. Was she playing him? Was he playing her? Should he just walk away?

His libido wasn't going to let him. Not until he'd had a chance to explore the sensuality she kept letting him get glimpses of. "I'm glad."

They finished up their lunch and made plans to meet later in the week, and Brian contented himself that he'd see her again soon at his offices. He knew that the best things in life took time.

Gracie Diaz had the kind of long, straight brown hair that Piper envied. She also had beautiful olive skin and big brown eyes. Piper smiled when she saw the woman she'd known since she was a girl. Gracie's father had done work for the Wingates until his untimely death. She'd recently had a huge lottery win and was now a mega-millionaire. Something that Piper suspected the other woman was still trying to come to terms with.

Gracie had been waitressing to put herself through

school and working hard to support her mom and brother over the years. After she graduated, Beth Wingate had offered her a job as her assistant and showed her the ropes of event planning. But now, due to her good fortune, she would never again have to worry about taking care of her family.

"Hi, Gracie," Piper said, giving the other woman a warm hug.

"Hello, Piper. The gallery isn't as busy as the last time I was in here," Gracie murmured.

"It's not. I think some people aren't sure how closely tied my gallery was with the Wingate companies. But that's not a problem. We're doing just fine. I spoke to Lauren and she mentioned that you were going to invest in the restaurant and help her decide on the art for your new restaurant venture."

"I am," Gracie said. "This is so exciting! For the first time in my life if I want to help someone, I can just do it. I love it."

"I bet." Piper smiled brightly. "I've pulled a few different paintings and some prints for you to look at, and we've set them up in the viewing room. Can I get you something to drink while we look at them?"

"I'd love some water," Gracie said.

"You got it," Piper replied. "Head into the room at the end of the hall. I'll be right there."

Piper entered the break room where Coco was eating a chimichanga that smelled strongly of chilis and seasoning. Piper grabbed two refillable water bottles that were monogrammed with the gallery's logo and headed out into the hallway where she noticed Gracie bolting toward the bathroom. Concerned, she closed the break room door and went after her.

From outside the locked bathroom door she could hear the other woman throwing up, then the sound of a flushing toilet. "Gracie, are you okay?"

The door opened and Gracie wiped her pale face with a towel. "Yes. I think I might have a stomach bug. Sorry about that."

"Here, have some water," Piper said, leading her into the viewing room and helping her take a seat. "I don't think we have anything bland to eat. There might be some butter cookies."

"I'm okay. The water is perfect," Gracie reassured her, looking at the paintings on the walls. "I love that longhorn image. Do you have more from that artist?"

"I do. I like it too. His work reminds me a lot of Ansel Adams's black-and-white photos. They are so evocative," Piper said. "I left the book of prints in my office. He's done some limited lithographic runs, so that's an option too."

She left Gracie looking at the other works they'd assembled in the viewing room and went to collect the artist's portfolio. She returned to find the younger woman standing under a picture that was titled *Broken Giants*. It was a photo of the oil derricks that dotted the landscape out toward Royal and Midland.

The land was vast and empty except for the derricks with the sun reflecting off the tops.

It was a very different image from the longhorn steers, but she could start to get an idea of the kind of subjects that Gracie liked.

"Do you like that?"

"Yes. It reminds me of how oil has given so many wealth, yet at the same time there is still all that land with nothing," she said.

"So true," Piper said. "Here is the first artist's portfolio. I have another artist who is doing something you also might like, but he's not established, and his art would be more of a risk than an investment. Do you want to see it?" she asked.

"Yes. I think Lauren and I both want the restaurant to have the right feel, and if the art is an investment that's great, but it's secondary to the feel of the images."

"Okay. Look through that while I find his work on my tablet," Piper said. They had a lot of different ways for their patrons to view the art that the gallery sold. As an artist herself, she got that. It was easier to represent herself through her art than to allow people to see the inner emotional part of her in real life. Safer, she thought. She knew that some of that was baggage from her past failed relationship, but it had felt less risky to let herself be free in the studio instead of with…men. Unbidden, a vision of Brian's sensual mouth drifted through her mind.

She shook her head, forcing herself back to the work. Some of the artists she'd worked with were more old-school and liked to send in slides that the gallery had to reproduce. Others sent in jpg images. She liked the variety because it reflected how the art and those who created it were all so different.

She and Gracie spent the next hour going over everything they had in the gallery that had the feel of the artwork that Gracie had been initially drawn to, and at the end of their meeting, Gracie had agreed to purchase several paintings and then asked for that new artist to come to the restaurant and create a custom piece for her.

Piper felt good as she wrote up the bill of sale and took the deposit from Gracie. Her business wasn't going to get back on track from one customer, but Gracie Diaz was proof that not everyone who was interested in art was from the same faction that had once rubbed elbows with the Wingates.

And, of course, she had the commission from Brian's building. She would make that work. Piper had always known that, as much as she loved making her living working with artists, the art world was a tricky business.

Brian. She had to remember they were working together, and as such, their relationship was strictly professional. Or was it…? She'd been way too giddy to see him in her gallery this afternoon. Brian stirred something inside of her that made her feel edgy and dangerous. But he was too young for her, and besides, he was Keith's nephew. Ava had a complicated history with his uncle, to say the least.

Which meant Brian was the last person she should be thinking of, but there was just something about him that Piper couldn't forget.

Three

Brian had several cases that were taking a lot of his time. The new clerk he'd hired was good but still making mistakes, and his uncle had called several times to talk about Ava Wingate. To say that Brian wasn't having a great day was an understatement. He needed a stiff drink and a night off, but he was holding a charity event for underprivileged children at the Mavs game tonight in his corporate box, so he still had work to do.

While he washed up in his private bathroom, he heard his assistant moving about his office. He came out with his shirt off since Tony was bringing in the new Dallas Mavericks jersey that he'd ordered to wear to tonight's game. His phone pinged and he glanced at the screen as he stepped into his office— it was a message from his uncle asking him to call. *Again.* He heard a sharp intake of breath and then a wolf whistle and looked straight into Piper's dark green eyes.

Her gaze drifted to his chest, making him start to harden. He flexed his muscles before he realized what he was doing, causing her to draw in her breath as she looked farther down his body.

Piper took a step closer to him and lifted her hand as if to touch him, but then she dropped her arm, shook her head and turned away.

He forced himself to go back into the washroom even though he wanted to move closer to her. See what she'd do next. However, he suppressed that urge because he was aware they were in the office and he had to act like a gentleman. He grabbed his dress shirt and pulled it on. "Sorry about that. I thought you were Tony."

"He wasn't at his desk and I knocked but came in. I should be the one apologizing, although I have to say, Cooper, that was a nice surprise."

He smiled at her and lifted one eyebrow. "Glad you liked it. Um, did we have an appointment tonight?"

"No," she said. "I was downtown at a meeting and thought I'd drop by and check out your offices."

"I'm happy to see you. I've got about thirty-forty

minutes before I have to be at the American Airlines Center for the Mavs game. I can show you around. Let me find Tony and then we can go. Do you want a drink?" he asked. "Help yourself to anything in the mini fridge."

Brian went back to his desk and pulled up the chat group for his executive staff. There was a message from his assistant saying he'd had to go down and sign for the jersey. He'd be back in ten.

Brian messaged him that he was showing Piper around and to leave the jersey in his office. Then he stood up as his phone pinged again. He looked down at the screen. Keith again. He was tempted to block him.

"Not a message you wanted?" she asked.

"No. Not really. It's from my uncle. He's at his wit's end now that your sister has moved out of his place," Brian admitted. "But I don't really want to discuss him."

"Me either," Piper said. "His actions aren't exactly the best lately. I'm not sure he didn't take advantage of Ava's grief."

Brian didn't know about that. His uncle had fallen hard for Piper's sister. From where Brian stood it seemed like his uncle's feelings had gone from friendship to something deeper and that Ava had encouraged that. Leading him to believe that there could be something real between them without any intention of ever following through. "I mean, he really loves your sister. I'm not sure how that is taking advantage of her. That would be—"

"I think it's probably best if we don't discuss this. You're going to naturally defend your uncle and I get that, but I don't want that to come between us. I like you, Brian."

He wished he could just walk away from Piper. For both their sakes. But he wanted her, and as he got to know her, he was starting to like her too. He felt as if he was in a better position than his uncle was with Ava because Brian hadn't always been secretly in love with Piper. Just in lust, he thought. Pursuing her wasn't the smartest course of action, but it was also something he had to do right now.

He wasn't sleeping because of his torrid dreams about this eclectic beauty, but he knew himself well enough to know that once he'd had her, his fixation on her would start to wane. She might be different from the other woman he'd dated, but *he* wasn't different. He was still more dedicated to his career and building his legacy than he was to starting a serious relationship.

"I like you too, Piper," he said, dropping the subject as she asked although he knew that Keith was always going to be between them because of his past with Ava. "As you can see, the atrium is huge and I was hoping to find something to fill it up. I was thinking either a sculpture or maybe a mural?"

She looked over the railing into the open space

outside of his office which was a big great space that was open all the way down to the lobby. There was a brass railing on one side that offered a view of the atrium and then on the other side had two couches and a bank of windows that looked out over downtown Dallas. "I like that idea. I think we'd have to commission a mural—I don't have that many artists I work with who do murals—but I do have a piece that might fit that space so you can look at that first." Pulling her notebook from her shoulder bag, she jotted down a few notes before stowing it back in her bag.

"Sounds good. I'm really in your hands. I just want the place to look good. To reflect our clientele and all the hard work I've done to start my own practice."

"I can definitely do that," she said.

Brian wasn't surprised. Piper was a woman who made things happen. He took her through all the other spaces and showed her the different spots he thought needed art.

"I have to leave when we get back to my office, but I want to get the paperwork rolling on this. Do you mind if I pass you off to my assistant?" he asked.

"Not at all," she said. "You're a big Mavs fan?"

"Yes, even when they aren't winning, but tonight I'm hosting an event," he replied, looking down into her eyes and realizing he didn't want their time together to end. Should he invite her to come along?

It seemed like the quickest way to see if they were going to hook up. But he also admitted that the more time he spent with her, the more this wasn't just about lust and ending his sexual torment about Piper.

"What kind of event?"

"I sponsor a program with the local elementary schools. If someone gets all As for the grading period, their name goes into a draw and I bring the winners to the game," he said.

"That's a great incentive," she murmured. "I wouldn't have expected this from you."

"Thanks. What did you expect?"

"Someone more driven to ensure his company's success at all costs," she admitted. "Taking care of kids like this is really the kind of gesture that helps to build their futures."

"I thought so. Also, some of these kids would never get to go to a game otherwise," he said as they reentered his office.

Tony stood there with a sheaf of papers in his hands and the look that meant that Brian had more things to do before he left.

"You have about ten minutes until you need to leave. I've got a car waiting downstairs for you, so you don't have to worry about parking. The charity has confirmed that ten kids and a parent and/or guardian will be there. They have one boy whose older brother would like to come I told them yes," Tony said. "Also, I need your signature on these."

"Thanks, Tony. Would you get Ms. Holloway's details and write up a contract for her to do the art for the building?"

"Yes, sir. Ms. Holloway, please have a seat," his assistant said.

"Of course," she replied. "See you later, Brian."

He hesitated. He was seconds away from inviting her, but he needed to get himself in hand before he did that. He was in lust with Piper. He wasn't about to start getting emotionally entangled with her. That was a complication that neither of them needed.

"Later," he said.

Piper curled up in her pajamas later that night watching the Mavs game and thinking about Brian and Keith. Were they the same type of guy?

She had spent a lot of time over the last five years decorating her house in Frisco, one of the northern suburbs of Dallas. She'd haunted estate sales and online auction houses to get everything right. Her goal was to purchase pieces that were solid and could keep up with her eclectic and changing tastes. Piper looked at the tribal art she'd purchased recently and smiled to herself. She'd been slowly updating her collection and the new goddess mask suited the new phase of her life.

A tinge of sadness flowed through Piper as she thought about Ava exiled from her own home and struggling to get her company back from the brink.

Piper wondered if there was some way she could help the Wingates. She had overheard some snippets of conversation at the wedding that suggested Keith might know more about the troubles at Wingate than he let on. He'd been helping out and making decisions for Ava while she'd been overwrought with grief for her husband.

If Piper had another reason to see Brian, would she feel safer somehow? Like she could go out with him because she knew she was doing it for her family. Though she wasn't involved with the business or really that close to Ava.

She started a group text with her family, wanting to ask them what kind of information from Keith they were looking for, but every time she tried to word her text it just sounded like she was Nancy Drew trying to solve a mystery on a bicycle. She had no idea how to get information from Brian. He'd brought his uncle up today, so she felt like she could easily ask him about Keith if she needed to, but she was stymied as to what she should ask.

Piper called her sister, but it was after nine and Ava's phone went straight to voice mail. She didn't leave a message. What could she say?

Rubbing the back of her neck, she headed to her studio. She had been spending more and more time in here lately. Her art had always provided an escape from the real world and this trying time was no different.

She was working on a second piece based on a spoken-word poem she'd heard at a café down the street from her gallery. The author of the poem was a nineteen-year-old man who'd spent most of his teen years in and out of juvenile detention, and the last time he'd gotten out they'd warned him he'd likely go to prison if he got in trouble again.

Xavier had challenged himself to find another life, but his poem spoke of the struggle to live within the law and not take it into his own hands. The idea for the sculpture had come to her one night while she'd been sleeping. She'd thought that would be enough for her. But she'd been called to the canvas and had been working on an abstract painting that showed both sides of Xavier. The intelligent young poet and the tough gang member who wouldn't hesitate to kill. She'd seen now they both existed inside the same man, the struggle constant as each side fought to remain in control.

Piper had asked his permission to use his poem and likeness for the sculpture, which she'd be donating to be auctioned off for Habit for Humanity at the end of the month. But she wanted to gift Xavier the canvas. She was almost finished with the piece. The figure had pen and paper in one hand, a gun in the other. His eyes were still haunting her.

She couldn't get the intelligence just right. Unbidden, an image of Brian's eyes as he'd talked to her about his building flashed into her mind. He had that inner core of intelligence and determination…that was what she'd been missing for this piece. She went back to work, furiously working until she stepped back and saw Brian's eyes in Xavier's face.

She was pleased with what she'd accomplished. Glancing down at her watch, she was surprised to see it was after midnight. She wandered out of her studio and noticed her phone was buzzing on the coffee table where she'd left it. Her heart skipped a beat when she saw it was a text from Brian.

Brian: I know you are probably sleeping, but I wanted to apologize for how I had to leave this evening.

Piper: Still working in my studio. You don't have to apologize. I dropped by unannounced. How was the game?

Brian: Dismal. I know we are in a rebuilding season, but tonight was painful.

Piper: I don't follow sports but…hugs?

Brian: [[Laughing emoji]] Thanks. What are you working on so late?

Piper: A portrait. It really needs to be finished but I was struggling to get it done.

Brian: Does that happen a lot? I don't think I ever realized that you were an artist.

Piper: It's not my main thing. It's just an outlet… sort of more hobby than occupation. I do a lot of collaborating.

Brian: I really liked the sculpture I saw at your gallery. I'd love to see some more of your work.

Piper: Maybe you will. [[Wink emoji]]

Brian: Maybe?

Piper: I mainly do commissions. This piece is a gift for a collaborator that I worked with for a charity auction.

Brian: Which one?

Piper: Habitat's Boots & Boas at the end of the month.

Brian: I have a table. Want to join me?

Yes, she thought. But was she being too impulsive? Her mind tried to reiterate all the reasons she'd been listing since she'd first danced with him about why spending time with him was a bad idea, but she pushed them aside. Piper had realized in her midthirties that she regretted the things she didn't do more than those she actually did. She had the feeling she'd always regret not going with Brian. Plus maybe she could information from him to help her family.

Piper: Yes. I have to get to bed now. Talk to you later about the art for your building.

Brian: I wish you didn't have to go. Good night, Piper.

Piper: Good night.

She put her phone down and went to shower before she did something impulsive like invite him over. There was still too much standing between the two of them for her to be this interested in him. She knew it, but she pointedly ignored that part. And besides, it wasn't as if this flirtation could develop into anything serious anyway. She was just going to take what she could with him and let that be enough.

He was fun and attractive. And, damn, the man was *ripped*. Piper never would have guessed that underneath his perfectly cut suits he was in such magnificent shape. She'd been trying very hard to forget what he'd looked like with his shirt off, but as she drifted off to sleep that night her dreams were filled with him naked and moving seductively over her.

Piper had been in and out of his offices for the last week, and Brian had caught a few glimpses of her but there hadn't been time to talk. He'd had a case that should have been handled in mediation go to court and it had been a hell of a fight. He was ready for Friday night when he walked into his office and saw Piper hanging a portrait on his wall.

She had on a flowy white blouse with the sleeves pushed up to her elbows and a pair of leather pants that made her legs seem even longer than he had noticed them being before. A few locks of her short dark hair were tucked behind one ear.

"Who's there? Tony?" she asked. "Come help me with this. I should have waited—"

"It's Brian," he said, hurrying to her side and taking the weight of the painting from her. "I got this."

Her cinnamony perfume made him think of

Thanksgiving and family. But the brush of her hip against his thigh conjured images of a long night spent burning up the sheets. He felt the portrait tremble in his hands, and he forced himself to get his urges under control. Shifting the portrait, he felt for the hooks on the wall and settled it onto them.

She turned toward him, her green eyes glazed with lust, and he realized that he was reaching the end of his rope. It felt like he'd waited years for her and right now, as she stood so close to him, smelling of cinnamon and looking like the only thing he'd ever wanted, he needed to kiss her. To taste her full mouth and see if the passion he'd felt from the moment they'd met was real or just a figment of his imagination.

The door was open, and he didn't want her to feel pressured so he took a step back and stumbled over the small toolbox he hadn't realized she'd left on the floor. She reached for him, her hand grabbing his forearm as he steadied himself, drawing her off balance. He caught her easily with one arm around her waist.

She put her hand on his chest and their eyes met. Something unspoken passed between them. Both of them were wary of pushing this and losing the chance of friendship. Or at least that was *his* concern.

"Thanks," he said. "Sorry for being so clumsy."

She didn't step back but stayed where she was

with her hand on his chest. "I think we both know that you aren't clumsy."

"I feel like it around you. I seem to lose all my chill with you, Piper."

She shook her head, worrying her bottom lip between her teeth, which made him close his eyes so he wouldn't be so focused on her mouth. He wanted to kiss her. *Needed* to, actually. He literally felt like if he didn't put his mouth on hers, he'd stop breathing, which he knew was ridiculous.

But with his eyes closed, the touch of her hand on his chest and the scent of her was stronger than his rapidly waning self-control. He was surrounded by Piper Holloway. The woman he couldn't stop thinking about. The woman he'd promised himself he'd let set the pace. He had to get away. He let go of her, opened his eyes and moved away from her. She watched him go and then wrapped her arms around her waist, turning to look at the portrait she'd hung.

He did the same. Anything to draw his attention from her lithe body and her sensual mouth. The portrait was a surprise. It was a version of the corporate photograph that he'd had taken earlier in the year. But this oil painting had somehow captured his energy and passion. He looked like a man who would conquer anything.

"Who did this?"

"I did," she said softly. "I hope you don't mind. If you hate it, I'll take it down."

"I love it. You flatter me with your rendition of me. But I wish I was that man," he said.

"You *are* that man, Brian. I was going to just hang the picture you had taken for the law journal but then… I haven't been sleeping and somehow found myself at the canvas. Anyway, this is a gift and not part of the commission to decorate the building."

He moved closer. Was this how she saw him? He hadn't been paying attention to her words but then they sank in. "I'm paying for it. I should have thought to have you do this earlier. But I hadn't seen any of your work."

He'd had the feeling she didn't want him to see her work and now he understood why. There was something very intimate about the way she'd painted him. And she'd revealed a bit of herself in the work as much as she had stripped away his outer layers, showcasing parts of him that he'd shown to her in conversations.

She'd really captured what he hoped to be. But it was an idealized version of him. Could he be that guy? Did he even *want* to be? She'd somehow seen through the outer man to the person he truly was.

Brian wasn't too sure he liked it. He didn't want anyone to see him this way—it made him feel vulnerable and he didn't want to be. But maybe that was because she made him feel that way? And perhaps, deep down, a part of him hungered to live up to what she saw in him.

"It's interesting. I like it," he said, knowing he couldn't say that she'd seen him in away that made him feel vulnerable.

She turned to face him, and he saw that questions lingered in her beautiful green eyes. She seemed nervous about his reaction. "Good. It's hard to gauge my own work. I always like it until I'm waiting to hear what someone else thinks, and then I just see the flaws."

He moved closer to her because he hated being even a few feet away. "I'm not just being nice. It's really good."

She turned then, and this time as their eyes met, a jolt of awareness sizzled between them. He knew he might regret it but he also knew he couldn't wait another moment to kiss her. To get a little bit closer to this complex, exotic woman who had turned his life upside down.

Four

Piper hadn't intended to be here when he saw the portrait. She'd spent too many nights working on it and pouring her sexual frustration into it. Sure, she wanted Brian, but they were busy people with very different lives, and she was old enough to know that just wanting a man didn't mean he'd ever be hers. So she'd painted him instead.

But now he was holding her in his big, muscular arms, looking like he wanted to kiss her but also hesitating, as if he didn't want to pressure her into anything. She put her hands on the sides of his face, felt that strong jaw and the stubble that wasn't visible as she went up on her tiptoes and brushed her lips over his.

An electric tingle went through her body and everything feminine inside of her screamed *it's about damned time*. The next time her lips grazed his, he took control of the kiss. His lips moving under hers, he angled his head and his tongue swept over her lips. Gently at first, and then demanding entrance so it could probe deep inside.

He tasted minty, and as silly as it might seem, *manly*. Brian held her loosely, never making her feel trapped, as he deepened the kiss. She slipped her hands down the sides of his face to his neck, caressing the tendons there as she slowly moved her touch to his shoulders. Piper knew how ripped and in shape he was. Felt the strength in his shoulders and in his arms as he lifted her slightly and turned so that his back was toward the open door of his office. She tore her mouth free of his and their eyes met. She didn't want this to end. There was something in his eyes that seemed to say the same thing.

Brian rubbed his thumb over her lips and another sensual shiver went through her all the way to her toes. Her lips felt too sensitive, full and hungry, she thought. She was hungry for more of him. More of his kisses and definitely more of him without his dress shirt on.

He sighed and stepped back from her, but not before she felt the brush of his erection against her thigh. "That nearly got out of hand."

"Nearly," she said softly. Knowing that she would have been very happy if it had. She was used to men who...heck, she wasn't used to *any* man. Truth was, she was leery of men, having been ill-used by her fiancé back in her twenties. And, as a consequence, she kept a wall up and kept her distance.

She moved back from Brian. She only had to look at the portrait to see what she felt for him. How much she wanted things from him that she knew weren't in the cards for her. She had no business kissing him, and not for any other reason than she was too old to have her heart broken by a ripped body and a mouth that made her forget her own name. Too old.

Too wise.

Ha.

She was supposed to be entering the wise goddess period of her life, but she felt as untried as she had felt at twenty-one. This wasn't going to work. Hook-ups were one thing, but...whatever this was—just no. She wasn't going to do it.

"Um, I've got to go." She saw her shoulder bag on his guest chair and started walking toward it, her own sense of panic growing. Not because of Brian but because he'd done something she hadn't expected. He'd awakened that feminine part of her that she'd shoved way down and tried to kill. And this was wrong...on so many levels. Because he sparked a desire in her for things that she knew she couldn't have. Things that still made her want to mourn.

"I'm sorry," he rasped. "I didn't want to push you."

She paused in the doorway and looked back at him. Even now it was all she could do to keep from closing the door and ripping off his shirt. Giving into the fiery passion that was coursing through her and making her hands shake.

Wise goddess.

She hoped that reminder would be enough.

"You didn't. I pushed and I shouldn't have. I'm not… I'm just not ready for this," she confessed. "I'm glad you like the painting. I'll be back with more pieces next week."

She turned to leave but he was there, his hand on her elbow, just the brush of his fingers against her arm, slowing her down. "How do you feel about dinner?"

She looked at him over her shoulder.

"To discuss the installation? I don't think we need to consult any more unless you don't like the pieces."

"I like them. I was asking you out…on a date," he said sardonically.

She had just pretty much decided it was more than passion in her mind, but he was making everything real by asking her for a date. "We can't date. I'm too old for you. You should find someone—"

He put his fingers over her lips and stopped her

from talking. "There is no one I want like I want you, Piper. If you don't want me, that's one thing. But our ages aren't a big deal. When we are together it's honestly not even something I've ever thought of. Please, come to dinner."

She looked up into his dark brown eyes and felt her will weakening. It had been just one kiss and she could control this attraction. She was a wise goddess not a sex-crazed woman. She had this under control. And, honestly, dinner sounded nice.

Better than nice. She hadn't been on a date in a long time. Partly due to the walls she used to keep men at arm's length, but mostly because she worked all the time.

"Okay. I'd like that. Where should I meet you?"

"How about CRU Food and Wine Bar in The Shops at Legacy?"

"8:00 p.m.?"

"Yes," he said. She turned to leave again and this time he pulled her back into his arms and pivoted them out of the doorway. He tipped her head back, kissing her again, and this time he held nothing back. And long breathless moments later, when he finally lifted his head, she didn't feel wise. She felt empty. Lonely. Unfulfilled. Like she'd had a taste of something she desperately craved and that made her hunger for so much more.

"See you soon."

She walked away, wondering if she'd just taken a reckless leap into the unknown.

CRU was an upscale Texas wine bar. They'd been the first to offer over thirty wines by the glass and had vino from all over the world and at every price point. They also had a relaxed atmosphere with Napa-style foods and delicious, wood-oven pizzas.

Brian had chosen it because it was close to her home and he knew the general manager. Working in the city had given him a great network of connections and he was glad tonight that he'd been able to secure a reservation through that. He didn't mind waiting for a table, but it was his first date with Piper and he didn't want to spend the time with her standing in the waiting area.

Plus, it was a relaxed atmosphere so there would be no pressure on either one of them. He wanted to be cool about this, but he knew himself and how he felt about this woman, and there was nothing chill about that. But tonight, he reminded himself, was about Piper. Her wants. Her needs.

And doing everything he could to make her feel comfortable.

But damn. That kiss…

That portrait she'd done of him had changed the game. He wanted to stay focused on the lust side of it, and boy had he gotten his wish. Because her kiss had made him want to make her come in his arms again and again until she was exhausted and she forgot about that man she'd painted.

But, in a way, that lip-lock had been the sweetest kind of torture too. Because the attraction between them wasn't something he wanted to walk away from and now he knew it with bone-deep certainty. That she'd started to walk away warned him he needed to be careful.

He'd been surprised when she mentioned their age difference. Because, to be honest, it was as he'd told her...he hardly noticed the eleven years between them.

Blowing out a breath, he tossed his keys to the valet and walked into the restaurant. He looked around the lobby for Piper and didn't see her so he gave his name to the maître d. A minute later Hugh—the owner—came over to greet him. They shook hands. "Good to see you, Brian, and not during billable hours."

Brian had to laugh at that. Hugh and his wife went through periods where they both wanted to divorce but they had never gone through with it. "It is nice. Thanks for helping me out tonight with a table."

"Not a problem. I'm guessing this was a last-minute date," Hugh said.

"Yes," Brian replied, not wanting to discuss Piper with the other man.

"Say no more. If you need anything let me know,"

Hugh said, as one of the waiters came to get his attention.

He walked away as the door opened and Brian turned to see Piper walk in. She wore a halter top under a black leather biker jacket, a pair of boot-cut black trousers and heels, and seemed to stand out from everyone else in the waiting area. Their eyes met and she smiled when she saw him.

He noticed the way everyone's gaze seemed to follow her and realized she didn't see that. Didn't realize how she drew attention just by being the woman she was. He wondered how much of it was down to what she'd said about Ava always wanting her to fit a different mold.

"Hello, Cooper," she said. "I hope you haven't been waiting long. I got stuck at a red light."

"Not long at all." He grinned. "Let me tell the hostess we are ready to be seated."

"You got a table?"

"Yes, the owner is a friend," he said. "This place is more popular than I realized when I first suggested it."

She nodded and followed him to the hostess station, and they were led to their table. The after-work crowd was changing to couples out for the evening. He put his hand on the small of Piper's back as they moved through the tables following the hostess— more to touch her than to guide her.

She didn't seem to mind it and he took comfort in

that. He had wondered earlier if he'd pressured her into the date, but she was here and not pushing him away. He knew that they still had a way to go, but this was the first step.

Brian wanted her to get to know him. So that his reassurance that their ages didn't matter wasn't something that would ever bother her again. Plus, he wanted her to realize she wasn't a novelty to him. He wanted Piper because she was *Piper*, not for any other reason.

They were shown to a high table for two in the back and he held her chair as she seated herself. Then he took the bar stool across from her. "Thanks," she said. "I hate these high stools. I always feel like I'm not going to be able to get down."

"I don't think they have a low—" he began.

"Stop. I'm being silly. Ava's told me more than once to stop complaining about bar stools."

Brian quirked a brow. "Do you go out with her often?"

"Not really. When we are in Royal sometimes. I tried to get her to go out when Trent was so sick," Piper said. "It was hard to see Ava go from being such a glamorous, feisty woman to sort of fading away as Trent's sickness lingered and then worsened."

"That did seem to put a strain on her. Uncle Keith said he tried to distract her. It was hard on him, losing his best friend," Brian said.

"I think it changed them both," Piper admitted. "Ava hasn't been the same since."

"To be honest, neither has Uncle Keith. I think he saw Trent's death as a second chance for him to step up and be the man Ava needed." Brian sighed. He hadn't really intended to talk about his uncle tonight, but Keith seemed to be on Piper's mind.

"Maybe. I think he took advantage of her grief," Piper said.

"Ava Wingate?" Brian asked. It was hard to think of Ava letting any man take advantage of her.

"Even a strong woman has vulnerabilities, Brian," she said, pointedly drawing the menu toward her and opening it up.

"Of course. I didn't mean to imply that she didn't. I guess I don't like to think of Uncle Keith manipulating her. I know he loves her."

"Fair enough. And I don't like it when other people point out how bitchy Ava can be," she said. "Besides, we aren't here tonight to talk about them."

"No, we're not," he agreed. "We're here to see if there is more than just a spark from one kiss."

By mutual agreement they kept the conversation off of Ava and Keith, and talked instead about sports—Brian's passion—art, which was hers, and movies. She wasn't sure how, but they managed to cover all of these topics and found they had a lot in common.

"Are you interested in going to a Cowboys game?" he asked. "I've got season tickets and I usually go with my college roommate but he's going out of town. You know they always play Thanksgiving Day."

"I don't want to seem like I was faking most of the earlier conversation, but I didn't know that. Do they play here in Dallas?"

"This year they do," Brian said. "What about it? My folks have a big family gathering at their house in Southlake. I should let you know we are diehard Cowboys fans."

"I wouldn't have guessed after you told me how Tom Hicks donated the land out here to build an elementary school," she quipped.

He blushed, which was cute and made her want him that much more. He was fun and easy to tease, and she could tell that family meant a lot to him, which made it harder for her to probe for information about Keith even though they'd agreed not to discuss him. She didn't want him to betray his uncle— unless of course Keith had done something suspect.

Which right now no one could seem to prove.

Every one of her nieces and nephews just didn't like Keith and thought there was something off about him. Ava had moved out of his place, and that should have pacified them, but it hadn't. Which was making her think that there might be more to their suspicions than just irritation at Keith for swooping in so soon after Trent had died.

"So I guess I was gushing."

"Yeah, just a bit," she said, "but I like it. I would love to go to that football game with you."

"Good. And we have the gala for Habitat. It seems to me we might be dating," he said.

"Do we have to put a label on it?" she asked, but secretly she liked the sound of that. *Dating.* She'd be part of a couple and not the odd person at the table. Which she had been for the last few months, as it seemed everyone except her had a significant other.

"No, I don't need a label. I just wanted to make sure you knew I was thinking about us in a serious way."

"How serious?" she asked. A part of her was afraid to let him in. She'd seen her own strong sister disappear inside of Ava's complicated relationship with Keith. Was there something about Cooper men that was overwhelming? Manipulative? Could she be getting in over her head with this hot, sexy man?

"Not too serious. This is only our first date," he said.

His answer was perfect. Again, was he just saying the right things to win her over? What would he want from her? Actually, she couldn't imagine a man who was better for what she needed than Brian. He was young and fun. The kind of guy who wasn't looking for more than a few nights in her bed. And that made her cautious. Brian was good at reading people; she'd read about that in an article that had profiled him the previous year. It was one of the skills that made him so good in the courtroom. Was he reading her now?

She shook her head, took another sip of her sauvignon blanc and refused to let her niggling doubts ruin her evening with him. Even if they were dating, it was casual. They weren't going to ever get serious, or at least not right away. She was a wise goddess, she reminded herself.

"Do you date a lot?" she asked curiously.

"I do my fair share," he said. "But I haven't been serious about anyone since I graduated law school. I have been too busy trying to get my career going."

She could see that. Brian seemed to her the type of man who wanted to give his all to everything he did, be it career or relationship. She took another sip of her wine and realized she was almost done with her second glass. The older she'd gotten, the easier it had become to drink more wine than she intended. She set her glass aside and reached for her water.

"And what about you? Do you date a lot?" he asked.

She shook her head. "Not really. My relationships tend to be more like this one. It happens when the right person comes along. Not because I feel it's time to date again."

He nodded. "I like that idea. I try to do the same thing, but my work requires a fair amount of socializing, and at times it's better to have someone on my arm."

"You need a corporate wife," she said. "Someone who can be your partner."

Even as she had the thought, she realized she'd said it out loud as a warning to herself. She needed to remember that, whatever else this was, she was an independent woman. Piper never wanted be Brian's social plus-one. *I just want to have fun,* she reminded herself. And as he'd said, this was just their first date. There was no reason to overthink this.

"I don't need anything," he said. "And I'm very happy where I am tonight."

"Me too," she admitted. "I think I should be finished with gathering the art for your building soon."

"Tony took me to see the other pieces you've put up and I have to admit I do like what you've done. He said that all of the pieces are on a three-month temporary display." Brian glanced at her with interest. "What is your thought behind that?"

"I want to make sure that the work suits your building. Once you see it daily, you'll be able to determine if you want to keep it or not," she told him.

"Good idea. Is that something you do with all of your customers?" he asked.

"It depends on the client. If they buy it at auction, then it's theirs, but if we work together to find a piece for their home then I do give them some leeway. And it's an exchange policy for the same art-ist's work. It's not a refund."

"That makes sense. Art is subjective, isn't it? Just like couples," he murmured.

"How do you figure?"

"Not everyone who looks like the perfect couple will be one," he said.

Five

When the meal ended, he didn't want the night to end but he'd asked her to dinner…that was all. He needed to keep his desires in check to avoid scaring her off.

The Texas sky was big and clear that night; the light pollution from Frisco usually made seeing the stars almost impossible. And he wished they were on his ranch in Royal. They could go for a ride and he'd show her the stars.

"Do you ride?" he asked as he helped her into her coat.

"I do. I'm not really good but I enjoy it," she replied. "Why?"

"Just thinking tonight would be perfect for a ride."

"Yes, but we're in Frisco," she said with a slight smile.

"We are," he admitted gruffly. "Want to take a walk before we head home?"

She shook her head. The Shops at Legacy were an outdoor mall area that mixed restaurants with retail outlets and a large city park. But she didn't want to walk in public with him. She'd wanted to be alone with him.

Brian had promised himself he'd be chill, so he forced a smile and comforted himself with the knowledge that they'd had a really nice time at CRU. He could handle that. He'd call in a few days and invite her out again.

"Fair enough. It's been a long week," he said. "Did you valet park?"

"No," she answered.

"I'll walk you to your car, then."

"Why don't you get your car and drop me off?" she suggested. "Then you can follow me to my home, and we can have a drink and I'll show you my studio."

He looked into her dark green eyes, searching for a clue as to what she actually wanted from him, but he didn't find an answer. He just saw interest, and honestly, that was enough for him. "Sounds great."

He got his car from the valet and drove Piper to hers. He followed her to the gated community where her house was and was waved through by the security guard after Piper spoke to him. Her house was a large stone abode similar to the one his parents had. It was too large for one person, he thought, but it was obvious to him as soon as he stepped inside that Piper liked the space and had made it her own.

"House tour or drink first?" she asked. "November always makes me want to curl up by the fire and drink Baileys."

"November makes me think of turkey and football, but I think I might like your idea better," he said.

She smiled at him. "I'll pour the Baileys if you get a fire started. I was thinking we could sit on the back patio by the fire ring," she said, nodding toward the French doors.

"I'm on it. I was an Eagle Scout."

"I'm not surprised," she said. "Be right out."

He let himself out onto her patio and easily found the seating area surrounding the fire ring in the back yard. The lights had automatically come on as he stepped outside, so he immediately saw the cord of stacked firewood near the built-in outdoor kitchen. The patio floor was inlaid tile and the design was very Texan in scope. A big bold vista with a large sun in the center that her fire ring had been built into.

He used some kindling to get the fire started and then slowly added one of the larger pieces of wood to it. Dusting off the chairs, he moved two of the padded seats closer to the fire with an end table between them. He glanced up as the door opened.

Piper had draped a heavy blanket scarf over her shoulders and had a tray with the bottle of Baileys and two glasses with ice in them on it. After he took the tray from her, she went to one of the cabinets and grabbed two plaid throws. He noticed they were monogrammed with her initials when she handed one to him.

"In case you get chilly. This is my favorite time of year," she said. "The nights are longer and it's not too horribly hot most of the time."

He watched her wrap the blanket around her shoulders and almost offered to pull her into his arms. They could share some body heat and he'd keep her warm. Just thinking about it aroused him.

"I don't think I have a favorite time of the year," he admitted. "I do love summer and fishing out on the lake. But that's not a time of year thing…that's just a fishing thing."

"Do you eat what you catch?" she asked.

He shrugged as she offered him a glass with two fingers of Baileys in it. Their fingers brushed and a shiver went through him. "Mostly release them. I like the sport of it."

He wanted to pull her onto his lap and show her what he really was in the mood for tonight. Piper. That's what he wanted and he was trying to be a good guest but the struggle was real.

"I find it sort of soothing to be out on the boat while other people are fishing," she confided. "I usually take one of my portrait books with me and sketch."

"How does that work? Do you have to have some sort of inspiration, or do you just doodle and it turns into something?" He grimaced. "I'm not creative at all."

"I don't believe you aren't creative, but it might not be in the traditional I-make-art kind of way. I bet you come up with unique ways to solve problems in your life all the time…that's being creative," she pointed out.

"You sound very passionate about this," he noted, taking a sip of his drink .

"I am. I hate when people act as if being creative is something only given out to a few of us. Everyone has that inside of them. It might not produce art, but that creativity is there in everyone's daily life."

He wasn't sure he agreed but he could see what she was saying. "I think that might simply be more our uniqueness."

"Fair enough," she said. "I'm afraid I get a bit zealous when it comes to anyone denying they can be creative. I think it's like anything else in life. If it was important to you, you would do it and then nurture that skill. Then you would be creative."

"I can agree with that," he said. "I see that all the time when everyone says I'm so focused. It's just because I know that if I'm not, I won't be successful. Focus has given me my career and I work at it. It would be easy to grab my phone and check in with work during the day, but if I'm working on a brief then I finish it first."

"I can see that about you." She flashed a smile. "You are a man who doesn't stop until he gets what he wants, aren't you?"

"I am," he said.

"And what do you want right now?" she asked, putting her glass down and shifting in her chair toward him.

"You."

Brian kept surprising her with his intelligence and his boldness. She'd had an idea of the man he was, but he pushed away those cardboard cutout images and replaced them with his broad shoulders, smoldering dark eyes and firm jaw. Inviting him back to her place hadn't been her plan, but the longer she'd spent with him, the more she wanted him.

That kiss in his office had dogged her all afternoon and evening as she'd waited for their date. She'd told herself to be the wise goddess, but right now she didn't want to. In her mind the wise goddess was ancient and had long gray hair that hung to her waist. She watched life instead of participating in it. And Piper freely admitted she wasn't ready to be that woman. She still felt young and vibrant, and Brian accentuated that.

He made her want give in to temptation, even though there were still alarm bells going off that he wasn't the right man for this moment in her life. But she'd never listened to that type of caution. She'd always been more of a leap-and-the-net-will-appear kind of gal. So she'd leaped by inviting him into her home, and now she craved him more than ever.

But was she prepared for what came next?

He set his Baileys glass on the table and shifted in his chair so that he was facing her. Both of his legs were on the ground in front of him and she couldn't help but smile when she realized he was wearing a pair of boots. She had gotten used to the men in Dallas being very urbane, not necessarily Texan gentlemen, but Brian had been born and bred in Royal and there was a big part of him that was a maverick.

"Boots?" she asked. "It's so not what I expected from you. How did I miss them at the restaurant?"

"It's Friday night," he said with a wink. "That's my night to get back to my roots."

"My daddy used to do that too. Get all duded up on Friday night and put on his boots and hat," she murmured. She hadn't thought about that in a long time. Her parents had both passed away when she'd been in her early twenties and Ava had stepped in to pick up the slack but she had her young family.

She still missed them terribly. This memory was an unexpected surprise, like a warm breeze.

"Mine too. He was a lawyer during the week, but on the weekend, he's just a good old boy," Brian said. "I guess I like to think I'm a bit like him."

"I bet you are. You're not really anything like your uncle," she mused.

He groaned. "I know. Keith is a Royal man through and through, but my branch of the family tended to like the big D."

"I can tell. You fit in here very well, but there is a part of you that's very Cooper of Royal," she said. "I see your rancher roots at times."

"Ranching is definitely in my blood," he admitted. "Yours too, right?"

"Yes," she said. "But not in *my* blood, per se. I mean, I liked the ranch, the wide-open spaces and finding a quiet place to hide and sketch. But the actual ranching parts…well, aside from riding, I don't think I'd make a very good rancher."

"Luckily you don't have to be." Putting his hands on his thighs, he leaned forward toward her "Do I unnerve you, Piper?"

Did he?

She wanted to say no, but a part of her acknowledged that would be a lie. After all, she'd asked what he was focused on and he'd said her. *Her.* Piper Holloway. The woman who'd walked a solo path for a long time by her own choice.

And she'd liked the idea of his focusing on her.

She tried to frame it in her mind that it was sex. Just the playing out of the kiss that had happened in his office, but she knew it was more. She didn't normally go out and she certainly hadn't invited a man back to her place in a long time.

"I don't know," she admitted. "You said what I was hoping you would, but now I'm not sure…"

Several moments of palpable tension passed between them. "Would you like me to leave?" he asked at last.

She was torn for a minute. There was so much she was unsure of, starting with trusting her own instincts when it came to him. But she knew he wasn't Keith. In fact, the more she got to know him, the less the two of them felt like each other.

"No," she said. "I don't want that at all."

"Then why don't we sit over there on the double lounger and watch the fire," he suggested huskily. "No pressure to do anything but enjoy this fall evening."

She looked over at him. Would that be enough? For another man it might not be, but she could tell from the earnest look on Brian's face that holding her while they fire crackled would be enough if it was what she said she needed.

Piper nodded. She got up and moved over to the big double lounger and maneuvered it closer to the fire. Meanwhile, Brian fiddled around with his phone until she heard some music start playing. It was George Strait. That native Texas son who seemed to always speak straight to Piper's heart.

The song was *"You Look So Good in Love."* An older song that was set to a country waltz. "My daddy used to love George Strait," he told her. "Want to dance instead of sitting?"

She remembered he had said he didn't like dancing. Yet right now he was holding out his hand to her. It was hard to resist the song *or* the man. She had been alone for a while by her own choice and she liked her life just fine like that, but tonight, with Brian, she was starting to realize that Brian had more to offer than she'd expected.

He put one hand on her waist and she put one hand on his shoulder and they joined their free hands. She didn't feel like he was trying to manipulate her. It seemed to her that he was just a guy holding a girl he liked. And she didn't analyze it more than that. She didn't want to worry that she was kidding herself as Brian sang under his breath and waltzed her around in a circle. Smart or not, all of her fears and reservations melted away.

She reminded herself that Brian was here only because she'd asked him. Sighing, she rested her head on his shoulder as he kept singing and dancing her around the patio. When the song ended, she looked up at him. A sizzle of awareness passed between them. Then he caught her jaw in his hand and rubbed his thumb over her lips.

Brian didn't want to rush her, but he could tell that Piper was having second thoughts. All of his life he'd been very sure of his path, but people were harder to manage, so he kept things cool and light because that was safer. He couldn't accomplish his goals if…if he let himself give into the emotions she'd stirred when he'd looked at that man she'd painted. He didn't want to be like his uncle Keith, devastated because of a woman. Brian wasn't that kind of man.

He dropped his hand and stepped back. He should never have put on George Strait. That man messed with his head and made Brian believe that his heart could be…well, something it wasn't.

"Thank you for the dance," he said gruffly.

"It was my pleasure," she said. "I get the feeling we are both overthinking tonight."

"Oh, yeah," he admitted. "I'm not going to lie, Piper, I didn't just start liking you at Harley and Grant's wedding reception. I've had my eye on you for a while now, which I'm sure you picked up on. And I want to be all cool about this, but I'm not. And something tells me that you aren't either…"

She watched him with that unfathomable gaze, and he wanted her to find whatever it was she was looking for on his face. But the harder he tried to project that, the surer he was that he looked like Ron

Stoppable from *Kim Possible*. That TV show he used to love as a kid. His mama always said that a person couldn't be what another person needed; they could only be themselves.

Be yourself.

But he didn't know if that man was what Piper needed…and he wanted her to want him. Not because he was ticking boxes and pretending to be the kind of guy he thought she wanted, but because the man he was would be enough for her.

"Oh, Brian. I can't let you just walk out of here," she whispered. "It might be smart. I hear what you are saying, and I know that those words are driven by my actions tonight, but I'll tell you one thing I've learned over the years…" She hesitated.

"What? Trust me, darling," he said.

She gave him that sad, sweet smile of hers. "I learned that I never regret being impulsive, but I always regret being cautious."

He pulled her back into his arms, but there was no music playing now. "I like that. I like *you*. I don't know if we will last more than this night, but I don't want to walk away either." He gazed deeply into her eyes. "So you really want this too?"

She nodded, as if words weren't going to be enough, and put her hands on either side of his jaw just like she had earlier in his office. He got instantly hard. Then he felt the warmth of her exhalation a moment before her lips touched his and it felt like his blood was running heavier in his veins.

Brian put his hands on her waist and lifted her off her feet and into his body, her stomach rubbing against his erection. Then she lifted one thigh and wrapped it around his leg. He pushed his tongue deep into her mouth because this kiss made him ravenous for her. Made him hungry for something that he could only get from Piper Holloway. Something that his cold and lonely soul had been hungry for.

He shifted around and moved until he felt the stone pillar of her patio at his back. Canting his hips forward, he let her rest against him. Their breaths mingled as her breasts pillowed against his chest and his hands moved up and down her body.

She tasted like Baileys and moonlight. Like the conversations they'd had and the ones that he wanted to have with her. Like every kiss he'd always wanted but had never had until this moment, and he knew he wasn't going to be able to ever just walk away from her.

This night would stay with him for the rest of his life and that felt right deep inside. He let his hands roam up and down her back, cupping her butt and drawing her more fully against him, rubbing the tip of his erection against that notch at the top of her thighs. She tore her mouth from his and her head dropped back as she took in a deep breath. He noticed the deep V in the halter top she had on and how her breasts rose and fell with each of her inhalations.

Brian drew one finger down the center of her sternum, tracing the gold circle charm that was nestled right above her cleavage before moving his hand farther down, grazing the side of her breast and feeling her heartbeat race as he did so. Their eyes met and he had no trouble reading the raw desire in hers.

He knew it must match the same in his own gaze. He lowered his mouth again, wanting to kiss her slowly. Wanting to take his time and make this moment last. However, needing her more than he needed his next breath, he knew that going slow was going to be impossible.

He wanted her spread out underneath him completely naked. And he also wanted to take her here against this post. To make her his so he could breathe again and then he could make love to her. Soft and slow and sweet. But first, he needed to claim her, with fierce unbridled passion, so that there would be no doubt as to what he wanted and who he was to her.

Six

Piper took his hand in hers and led him away from the post back to the big double lounger that she'd moved closer to the fire. This night was the kind that she'd missed. Companionship and sexy times were one of the few things she regretted about her choice to live her life on her own. But tonight, that wasn't a concern. Brian was here and doing things to her that she'd missed for such a long time.

She pushed him down and he leaned against the back. Emboldened, she climbed onto his lap, settling herself over his erection and rubbing her center over him. The low groan he let out made her breath catch in her throat. Then he cupped her butt in his hands, rubbing against the boot cut trousers she wore. She put her hands in his thick hair and tipped his head back. Then forced herself to close her eyes because she didn't want to think any more about what she saw on his face.

She just wanted to *feel*.

Life had been more than a little stressful lately and she needed this evening with Brian. He was complicated but so damned hot that she was just going to overlook the other parts. Just enjoy every second she had with this man. She loved the strength in him. He wasn't someone who was trying to pretend he didn't want her. Every movement of his body drew her closer to him. Made her want him even more. If she was so hungry for him, she should take her time, but she needed him.

Inside her.

Now.

His jaw had stubble on it and she liked the way it abraded her fingertips as she rubbed them over his skin. And that mouth of his, so wide and sensual with his full lower lip that just beckoned her closer, was too much to resist. She shifted up on his lap and his hands slid under her halter top, his large palm warm against her back as he splayed it against her skin.

She shuddered and brushed her lips over his and then angled her head to the side as he thrust his tongue into her mouth. Sucking on it, she drew it deeper inside, then felt his fingernail scraping along the base of her spine. She shivered again and lifted her head to look down at him.

"You feel even better than I imagined."

His eyes were heavy lidded—half-closed—and his lips were swollen from their kisses. There was a slight flush under his skin and his breathing was heavy. She pulled the halter top she had on up and over her head, tossing it aside. His eyes went wide open as he looked at her full breasts in the lace-covered bra.

"Fair enough," he said. "You are even sexier than in my dreams and they were pretty hot."

"How hot?"

He cupped her left breast with his free hand, his thumb rubbing over her nipple until it was taut. She shifted her shoulders and he fondled the fullness of her breast as she shifted forward, nudging his lips with her nipple. He licked her through the bra and sucked it into his mouth.

"Like Texas in the middle of August," he said, against her skin. "But hotter."

Piper moaned and spread her thighs so she could sink down on his lap and feel the ridge of his erection between her legs. She rocked her body against him as he continued to lave her nipple. He reached for the fastening of her bootcut pants and undid it, pushing his hand inside the back, under her panties, to cup her butt and drive her harder against him.

Throbbing with pleasure, she rode the ridge of his cock. She wanted more. *Needed* more from him.

"You are," she said.

God, it had been so long since she'd felt this good in a man's arms. She reached for the buttons of his shirt and tore them open, pushing the material aside so she could dig her nails into the firm muscles of his pectorals. He flexed them, the hand on her ass squeezing her cheek before he wrapped his arm firmly around her waist and rolled them over. He held himself above her and she felt his hot breath fan against her face. His chest was bare, with a light dusting of hair, and she couldn't help running her fingers over it.

Then, with his eyes burning into hers, he pulled the strap of her bra down her arm until her breast was free from the fabric and did the same with the other side. She lay underneath him, aware that she wanted him more than she wanted her next breath, and reached between their bodies to caress his erection through the fabric of his jeans. He groaned, capturing her wrist and drawing her hand up to his mouth. Then he kissed it and held it loosely next to her head on the cushion.

"What are you doing?" she asked.

"Trying not to come in my pants," he said, his voice coarse and gravelly.

She almost laughed at how good those words made her feel. "I don't want it slow—"

He put his hand over her mouth. "Woman, I'm hanging on to my control by a thread," he admitted.

Piper licked the palm of his hand and watched his pupils dilate as he moved it and brought his mouth back down on hers. She felt his hand stroking down her body, sliding underneath her to undo the clasp of her bra, and then she felt it being shoved down her arms. A moment later, she pulled them free to tangle her hands in his thick hair.

She shifted, parting her legs to try to rub her aching center against his hard-on. He groaned again and she felt his hand between their bodies working at the button fly on his jeans. She brushed his hands away to take over the task.

Brian shifted out of her grasp, though, pulling her pants down her legs and cursing when they got caught on her shoes. He turned to take them off and she sat up, gliding her fingers down his spine. Then she reached around his front to feel his erection. She stroked him, undoing the rest of his buttons before pushing her fingers into the opening of his jeans and taking him in her hand. He was hot and hard.

Brian shifted around, moving delicately to make sure that he could get Piper's hand out of his pants and not harm himself. He hadn't been this horny since he'd been in his early twenties. She got to him faster than he wanted to admit. He shifted around and looked up her body. She lay back against the cushion, her arms up above her head, her thighs slightly parted. Watching him with that direct gaze that almost seemed to dare him to look away. He couldn't.

He wanted her totally naked and she was, except for that tiny pair of red bikini panties. Lifting her with one arm around her waist, he slowly drew the silky material down her legs and tossed it aside. Then he stood up next to the chair and toed off his boots. It took longer than he wanted it to, but he didn't want to stop looking at the goddess in front of him.

He looked down at his shirt. "You've ruined one of my favorite shirts."

"I'll buy you another one," she said with a wink. "It was kind of your fault for being so ripped."

He shook his head. "Fair enough."

He'd never had a woman compliment him so often on his physique, and while he admittedly worked out to relieve stress and to keep his mind focused, from now on he thought he'd always think of Piper when he did. Brian tossed his shirt aside after undoing the buttons at the wrists and then pushed his pants and underwear down his legs, stepping out of them.

"Are you on the pill?" he asked. His voice was gruff again because she'd reached out to cup his balls as soon as he was naked.

"I am," she said. "I use it to regulate my period."

"Great." He was glad he didn't have to use a condom, unless she wanted him to. "I don't have a condom, but I'm clean."

"That's fine," she said. "I am too."

It was a conversation that he never felt awkward about having. They were in a new relationship, and it was the responsible thing to do.

"Now that we have that out of the way... I'm going to learn every inch of your body," he rasped.

"I like the sound of that," she said. "As long as I can explore too."

He realized he was going to have to keep himself under control because he wanted that, as well. Mutual pleasure had always been his goal when making love to a woman and tonight was no different. He crawled back onto the double lounger next to her after snagging one of the thick fleece-lined blankets, draping it over them so she didn't get cold.

Turning on his side, he drew her into his arms, kissing the side of her neck and slowly moving his way down the curve to her shoulder. Her cinnamon-scented perfume was a bit stronger there and he licked at the spot, tasting her skin. Then he moved lower, realizing that she had a tattoo on the inside of her forearm that he'd never noticed before. He shifted back so he could see it more clearly.

It was roman numerals in a classy font. He struggled to convert them to numbers but soon realized they were for the year 2001. "What is this for?"

As he ran his finger over the tattoo, gooseflesh spread down her arm and her nipple tightened.

"My annus horribilis. Just a reminder to myself that I made it through a year that I thought would kill me."

He turned his head, saw the shadows in her eyes and kissed her. "I'm glad. I bet it made you stronger."

"It did," she admitted. "Every time I see it, I stand a little taller, knowing I can handle anything that this crazy life throws at me."

Brian traced it again—he'd seen the steel in her more than once and knew that she'd have been shaped by her experiences. He wanted to know what had happened, but didn't ask. Instead, he resumed making love to this woman who was consuming him, body and soul.

Turning her on her side, facing away from him, he drew her back against his chest. He kissed her shoulder again, his hands cupping her breasts as he rubbed his erection between her butt cheeks. She shifted her legs, draping one thigh over his and pulling his top hand down her body and between her legs.

Brian cupped her in his hand, tracing over her center until he parted her and felt the tiny nub that was her pleasure center. He tapped it and she moaned a low deep sound and pulled his hand back, but she pushed herself against him.

"I liked that," she breathed.

He did it again, lazily plucking at her other nipple while dusting kisses along her back and tapping her clit. She writhed in his arms and he shifted his hips, rocking himself against her, causing her to gasp in pleasure. Then she reached up to push her fingers into his hair, and he brought his mouth hungrily down on hers as he drove her toward her climax.

Her nails rubbed against his scalp as her hips gyrated faster against his hand and his hard-on. He wanted to shift and enter her but he also wanted her to orgasm first. Wanted to see her body go tight and as she came.

She started making tiny sounds, quick and fast, and then she tore her mouth from his and screamed his name as her body spasmed in his arms. He held her, stroking her between her legs until she turned in his arms and pushed him onto his back, straddling him.

Brian felt her hand rubbing up and down his cock. He jerked forward and realized his control was more slippery than he'd imagined. Watching her orgasm in his arms had almost sent him over the edge. He was trying to make this good for her, but he wanted her so badly that he only had to think of the moisture between her legs to feel himself careening over the edge.

He had been laboring hard to get his own law firm off the ground. Working cases and overseeing the construction of his building had consumed his time and hadn't really left him with the chance to do more than hook up. But this was way more intense.

Because it was Piper.

Pleasure surged through him as she trailed her hand up and down his length, her fingernails scraping over his skin. Then, scooting backward, she came up on her knees to look at him.

She took his shaft in one hand, stroking him in her fist. Moving it up and down in a slow and sensuous movement that made his balls tighten. She skimmed her finger over the tip of his erection when she reached the top, and his hips jerked forward.

Cupping his sac in one hand, she squeezed very softly as she tightened her grip on his shaft, causing him to start thrusting in her hand. Then she leaned forward and he felt her breath on his erection a moment before her tongue dashed out and traced the tip of him.

Awareness moved through his body, making him hyperaware of her hand on his shaft. He meant to stay still, but tangled his hands in her hair as her mouth engulfed him.

She sucked on him, her hand fondling his balls, and he felt his control shatter, but he wanted to be inside her the first time they made love. He gently lifted her from him, and she kissed his shaft as she straightened up, looking him right in the eyes. "Too much?"

"Yes. I want to come inside of you," he said, his

voice sounding rough and gravelly to his own ears. Like all of the sophistication he'd cultivated over the years had been ripped away. "I don't want this to feel like something I imagined later."

"You imagine blow jobs?" she teased.

"Don't. Don't make me laugh right now," he gritted out, but he loved that she was so free and fun to be with. He lifted her onto his lap and lay back as he put his hands on her hips, thrusting upward until he felt her hot, humid core against his tip.

She smiled at him as she shifted around until he was inside of her, then lowered herself slowly, inch by delicious inch. When she was fully seated on him, she wriggled her eyebrows. "Is this what you had in mind?"

"No," he said, as he put one arm in the center of her back and drew her even farther down. Then, while he anchored her hips to his with his other hand, he drove himself up inside of her. Going as deep as he could. "This is."

"Oooh, I like it," she murmured.

Brian took everything she had to give him, pushing himself hard until he felt his orgasm shivering down his spine. His balls tightened and he heard those tiny sounds she'd made before her orgasm earlier as he let out his own roar and came inside of her.

He kept thrusting up into her until he was empty and then he fell back against the cushions, holding her in his arms. She rested her head in the curve of his neck and petted his chest as they both caught their breath. He rubbed his hand up and down her back, remembering that he'd said earlier they were simply dating. That this couldn't be serious since they'd only had one date. But he knew deep inside that was a lie. This was more serious than anything he'd experienced before. He held her lightly because he wanted to wrap himself around her and make it so he never had to let her go.

But he knew he had to. She didn't want anything serious with him. She'd pretty much said that. So he had to tread carefully.

For both their sakes.

"That was amazing," she said, lifting her head. "Want to spend the night?"

Brian looked up at her. He wanted so much more than that, but he could start with one night. "I'd love that. I have my gym bag in the car... I didn't get to work out today. Let me go and grab it so I have some clean clothes for the morning."

She nodded. "I'll clean this all up and meet you inside."

He pulled his jeans on and looked back at her, lying on the lounger with just the blanket pulled up around her body, her shoulders bare, and he knew he had found something that he hadn't been looking for. He didn't let his mind go there because only time would tell if his gut was right. Instead, he walked through her house and got his gym bag from the car.

Then he showered with her and made love to her again before they both fell asleep in her queen-sized bed. He woke often to look down at her. He'd somehow ended up in the one place he'd wanted to be, and it was both better than he'd expected and a hell of a lot scarier. He'd never been a man to run from anything, but the way Piper made him feel…he didn't want to dwell on it.

The next time he woke it was to the smell of coffee and the sound of Piper talking to someone in the other room. He walked out to find her sitting in her favorite armchair and talking on the phone. She looked up, putting her finger over her lips in a shushing motion.

"I'll call you back," she said, hanging up.

Was she embarrassed to have been with him?

Brian looked at her sitting there, the woman he had wanted for a while now. He'd always been the kind of man who was very good at getting what he wanted, and wasn't afraid to go after the things that might seem out of reach to others. He'd never thought of himself as *less than* until she'd motioned for him to be quiet.

He wasn't embarrassed to be here with her. But he realized that, as much as he might not view them as opponents, she did. She was squarely on her sister's side and she might not want Keith Cooper's nephew in her bed. And while that was her decision and he'd respect it, he didn't want her to have used him the way that it seemed Ava had used his uncle.

Seven

"What was that about?" Brian asked.

His hair was tousled from sleep, and seeing him this morning, looking sexy as sin, just reinforced all the feelings she'd had for him last night.

God he was so ripped that she had a hard time tearing her gaze from his chest. She felt that tingle in all the right places and wished she'd stayed in bed with him this morning. But he confused her. They should be casual but she'd awoken and stared down into his face, feeling something more.

Something that was far from casual.

Piper had always kept things light in her relationships because of her own self-preservation. She'd made up her mind after her broken engagement that she'd never be that vulnerable to a man again. Which posed a huge problem. Because she hadn't realized until this very moment that Brian meant more to her than she had thought he would.

"I just didn't want to have to explain to Ava that you had spent the night," she said.

"Explain? Why would you?" he asked, coming closer to her.

She was having a hard time keeping her eyes off his broad, muscular chest. He wore a pair of boxer briefs and nothing else. He had no tattoos on his body, was one-hundred-percent eye candy. Not a bad way to start the day.

Then his words sank in.

"She's was always mothering me. I think it's the age difference."

"Would you have asked any man to be quiet or is it just me?" he asked her.

She was beginning to realize that Brian was upset about this. "Anyone. Why? Do you think it was only you?"

"Yes. I'm younger. I'm Keith's nephew. I don't know if I was just some booty call for you or not," he admitted stiffly. "And shushing me…well, the last time I shushed a lover, I was sixteen and my dad was knocking on the door."

Piper arched one eyebrow at him. She wanted to know more about that story, but this wasn't the time. "Ava has always grilled me about every man I see. And this morning, when I'm here with you and happy, I simply didn't want that. I wanted to enjoy this Saturday morning, Brian, that was all."

He nodded and she got up from where she'd been sitting and walked over to him. Wrapping her arms around him, she gave him a kiss. Then, to her relief, he sighed hugging her back. "I know you're too good for me. I mean, Ava will probably tell you that."

"I don't care what she says. This is between you and me," she said firmly. "Now, do you want some coffee?"

"Yes," he answered. Then his stomach growled, and he blushed.

"Maybe some breakfast?"

"Yes. But you don't have to cook. I'll make us omelets," he said.

"That'd be great if I had eggs but I'm out. I do have toaster waffles and maple syrup. Will that do?"

"Definitely," he murmured.

She led the way into the kitchen and handed him a mug before pointing him to the French press that she used for her morning coffee. It was better for the environment than those capsule machines and she liked the taste of it better. She pulled a box of toaster waffles from the freezer and looked inside. There were three left. He looked like the kind of guy who would need more than one or two.

She put the three she had in the toaster and then

started going through her pantry until she found a can of fruit cocktail. "I'm so not prepared for overnight guests."

"I don't think either of us anticipated this," he said. "I don't regret it."

"I don't either," she admitted.

His phone started ringing in the bedroom and he took his coffee with him as he went to retrieve it.

Piper thought about Ava, who had called early wanting to talk. She'd have to call her back; there had been a note in her sister's voice that she hadn't heard since Trent got sick. Like she was edgy and depressed. Never a good combination in Ava.

"That was a client. I'm going to have to go," he said as he came back into the kitchen. "I wish I could stay for breakfast. Do you want to try to have brunch tomorrow? I'm going with my parents."

Parents? Not sure she was ready for that, she shook her head. "I can't. But I'll see you on Wednesday for the Boots and Boas Gala."

"Do you want to plan to stay at my place downtown?" he asked. "It's closer to the gala and you won't have to drive home after."

Piper liked how he'd made it seem logical; he was being chill about them and that made it easier *and* harder for her. She wanted to pretend he was just a hot younger guy she was sleeping with, but her emotions were already going wild. She nodded. "I'd love to."

"Sorry to have run out like this," he said.

"It's okay. It's your job."

He had put his jeans on and a black Under Armour T-shirt that she guessed had been in his gym bag. Piper followed him to the door, and he bent to kiss her before he left. She stood there in the doorway, watching him leave, until she realized she probably looked like a fifties housewife and closed it.

Piper liked Brian but he was bringing things to the surface that she knew couldn't ever be. She didn't feel safe being the sensual woman that he stirred to life. That woman was reckless and ruled by passion instead of logic. She'd been burned so publicly all those years ago and that was why she'd stayed single.

She rubbed the back of her neck as she felt the worry get the best of her. Why did what had transpired between her and Brian the previous night bother her? she wondered. But deep down she knew the reason. It was because the sensual, feminine goddess inside of her had been broken.

Perhaps irrevocably.

Which meant she should be very careful about what else went on between the two of them. As bad as thinking about her inability to let go and indulge in a relationship with a man eleven years her junior was, talking about it with him would be a million times worse.

Sighing, she went back into the kitchen as the waffles popped up. And though she normally limited herself to one, she put butter on all three of them and smothered them in syrup. She enjoyed her breakfast, telling herself she didn't mind eating alone, but in her heart, she knew she wished he was still there with her.

Brian spent the rest of Saturday taking care of one of his clients whose son had gotten arrested on Friday night. That was not his area of expertise and he brought in one of his former employers who did handle criminal law to handle it. By the time he had a chance to text Piper, it was almost six in the evening.

Normally he didn't overthink his relationships, but as he opened their text string, he knew he didn't want to come on too strong. Despite what she'd said about Ava, a part of him wasn't sure that she was okay with him as her lover. And he wanted to be so much from her. She was still hiding something from him.

But what?

And as much as he'd thought that sleeping with Piper would lessen his need for her, that hadn't happened. In fact, it had simply made him crave her even more.

Hell.

He'd never been a man to hesitate when he wanted something, and he wasn't going to now that he had a chance with Piper. He texted her to see how her day had gone.

Then he put his phone down and went to shower and get dressed. He usually went to the Texas Cattleman's Club in Dallas for dinner if he didn't have plans. And tonight wasn't going to be any different.

He put on his watch and then allowed himself to glance at his phone. She'd texted him back.

Piper: I ended up in my studio and started a new project. It's going well. How about you?

He sat down on the leather wingback chair in his bedroom, then responded.

Brian: Busy day for me but we got things sorted. Are you tired after working in your studio all day?

Piper: Yes. But also exhilarated! I know I said no to seeing each other tonight but I need to get out of my house.

Brian: I was going to head to the TCC for dinner. Want to join me?

Piper: Yes. Thank you. See you in about an hour?

Brian: [[thumbs up emoji]]

He smiled to himself, anticipating seeing her when he hadn't expected to. Was he letting himself get in too deep with her? Was she going to push him aside the way Ava had Uncle Keith? But he had never been able to control his emotions. He didn't fall easily for women, but when he did, it seemed it happened quickly.

He finished getting ready and then called an Uber

to the club. He figured he'd be drinking tonight and didn't want to risk driving home. When he got there he saw some new members he didn't know and a few people from legacy families, like his own, who'd belonged to the original Texas Cattleman's Club in Royal. He nodded to the people he knew but kept moving toward the bar. There he ordered a Lone Star beer and found a seat that gave him a view of the entrance.

He caught up on emails and sipped his beer, looking up every time the door opened until finally he saw Piper standing there. She smiled and waved when she saw him. Her pixie cut was styled in a punk-rock look tonight, and she wore a brown suede skirt that ended midcalf and a cream-colored sweater that ended at her waist. How did she manage to take his breath away every time she entered a room?

Piper headed over to him and he got up to hold a chair out for her. She took his hand and gave him a quick kiss before she sat.

"What can I get for you? I put my name in for a table but there's a forty-minute wait," he said.

"Skinny margarita," she murmured. "Maybe some nachos."

"Got it."

He walked over to the bar and placed the order, getting another beer for himself. It was too early in the evening for tequila for him. Carrying their drinks back, he set them down on the table and slid into a seat across from her. He wanted to hear all about her day but tried to play it cool.

She took a long drag on her margarita and sighed. "I was consumed with an idea after breakfast this morning. I thought I'd just do some sketches, but it turned into a full-blown concept and the next thing I know, it's nighttime and I'm starving."

"Does that happen a lot?" he asked with interest.

"Not as often as I'd like, but when it does, I just go with it," she said. "Does that happen to you?"

"Not the same way, but I think so. Sometimes I'll start doing research for a brief and the next thing I know it's midnight," he admitted. He'd always been called obsessive about his work but most of the time he just lost himself in it. He liked uncovering the path to justice for his clients. Finding and noting precedents were one of the things he'd always loved.

"That sounds exactly like it. I was starving when I finished, and as you know there is no food in my house," she said ruefully. "I pretty much pick up something to eat every night on my way home from the gallery, but I've been so busy with the extra work I've taken on."

"Hopefully you can slow down soon," he murmured as their nachos arrived.

"I hope so, but I'm not sure what it will take to change people's minds. You know how small-minded they can be sometimes."

"I do," he admitted. There were a lot of people

who thought that where there was smoke, there was fire where the Wingates were concerned, but he'd known that family for a long time now and they were upright people. Not lawbreakers. "I hate that you are being affected by it."

"Me too. I worked hard to establish the gallery, but now everyone wants to believe that I took tainted money," she said, shaking her head. "I don't want to talk about that tonight. Tell me about your day."

He distracted her by talking about how he'd had to be more therapist than lawyer for his client while a colleague took over the case. He couldn't go into specifics, due to lawyer/client privilege, so switching gears, he started telling her about a new modern art exhibit that he'd heard was coming to Dallas.

Somehow after dinner she found herself agreeing to play a game of pool with Brian. She hadn't played since college, when she'd hustled guys who used to hit on her and her roommate, Char, when they went out. Her first shot was wide and not very good, so she wasn't too sure that she was up to this hotshot attorney's level.

He hadn't missed a shot until she noticed that if she bent over her shot, he watched her and not the ball. And though it probably wasn't fair of her to do it, she started using it to her advantage. Which was great for getting her a turn, but she still hadn't sunk a ball.

"You know what might help?" he asked as she lined up for her next shot.

"Hmm?"

He came up behind her. His hips fitted to hers and then he leaned over her. Putting one hand on the green felt and the other on her shoulder, he scolded, "If you stopped trying to distract me and actually paid attention to your game."

She turned and wrinkled her nose at him. "Distracting you is the only thing I'm good at tonight."

He laughed and stood up next to her. "How long has it been since you played?"

"At least fifteen years," she replied. "And I did okay back then."

"Did you do a lot of distracting?" he teased.

"Believe it or not, I thought that was crass behavior and never tried it," she said. "Usually guys would go easy on me and Char because they thought we couldn't play. All we had to do was a get a turn and we'd sink them all."

"So, you were pretty good then," he said.

"We were okay. But you, my friend, have real skills."

"My dad has a table and we played at home," he admitted. "I like it. It forces me to get out of my head. My dad always says I can't debate a ball into seeing things my way."

She had to laugh at that. As free-spirited as she was, Brian seemed equally intense. He was a man who spent his days thinking and arguing and winning people around to his way of thinking. She had to remember that. He was very persuasive.

"Since you are killing me at this game, what do you say we stop playing?" she suggested.

"I don't know. I like it when you pretend to drop something just as I line up a shot," he said.

She threw her head back and laughed. "I'm willing to keep doing it at your place."

"You want to come home with me?"

"I do," she said softly. "If you want me to…"

"Hell, yes." He took her hand and drew her into his arms, looking down into her eyes. She realized how well they fit together. And while she still had her guard up, she decided to stop worrying needlessly over this thing with Brian. She needed someone in her life who got her and let her be herself. Someone who was on her side, and Brian seemed to be that man.

"Do you want to finish your drink?"

"I'm good," she said. Honestly, she just wanted to be with him. All day long she'd been working on a painting that summed up her life right now. It was abstract, but people had started to emerge as she'd worked. Her sister, of course, her daddy, to whom she'd always been close…and then Brian. The more she'd worked on the painting, the clearer it had become that she wasn't going to be able to just label him as a distraction. He was already deeply rooted inside of her.

So, she'd decided to go with this for as long as it lasted.

"Let's go," he said, leading her out of the billiards room and outside. "I took an Uber, did you drive?"

"I did," she said. "It's damn expensive to get an Uber from Frisco."

"Do you mind leaving your car here overnight?" he asked. "I've had too many drinks to drive."

"I don't mind at all," she said. The parking area was monitored, and she didn't want to take a chance on either of them driving after drinking.

He called an Uber and they were in his penthouse apartment before she knew it. The place was modern, yet had a homey feel to it. He led her into the living room and she admired the view of the glittering Dallas skyline as he made them margaritas in the other room. She took off her boots and wondered what she was doing there, but knew there was no other place she wanted to be.

That thought scared her. So much so, she was seconds away from getting her stuff and leaving.

He came back with two margaritas and handed one to her. "What would you like to do?"

Cuddle on the couch and watch TV, she thought. But she didn't dare say that out loud. She had warned herself against this. He was becoming too important

Get Up To 4 Free Books!

Dear Reader,

IT'S A FACT: if you answer 4 quick questions, we'll send you 4 FREE REWARDS from each series you try!

Try **Harlequin® Desire** books featuring the worlds of the American elite with juicy plot twists, delicious sensuality and intriguing scandal.

Try **Harlequin Presents®** Larger-Print books featuring the glamourous lives of royals and billionaires in a world of exotic locations, where passion knows no bounds.

Or TRY BOTH!

I'm not kidding you. As a leading publisher of women's fiction, we value your opinions… and your time. That's why we are prepared to reward you handsomely for completing our mini-survey. In fact, we have 4 Free Rewards for you, including 2 free books and 2 free gifts from each series you try!

Thank you for participating in our survey,

Pam Powers

To get your 4 FREE REWARDS:
Complete the survey below and return the insert today to receive up to 4 FREE BOOKS and FREE GIFTS guaranteed!

"4 for 4" MINI-SURVEY

1 Is reading one of your favorite hobbies?
☐ YES   ☐ NO

2 Do you prefer to read instead of watch TV?
☐ YES   ☐ NO

3 Do you read newspapers and magazines?
☐ YES   ☐ NO

4 Do you enjoy trying new book series with FREE BOOKS?
☐ YES   ☐ NO

Please send me my Free Rewards, consisting of **2 Free Books from each series I select** and **Free Mystery Gifts**. I understand that I am under no obligation to buy anything, as explained on the back of this card.

☐ Harlequin Desire® (225/326 HDL GQ3X)
☐ Harlequin Presents® Larger-Print (176/376 HDL GQ3X)
☐ Try Both (225/326 & 176/376 HDL GQ4A)

FIRST NAME	LAST NAME

ADDRESS

APT.#	CITY

STATE/PROV.	ZIP/POSTAL CODE

EMAIL ☐ Please check this box if you would like to receive newsletters and promotional emails from Harlequin Enterprises ULC and its affiliates. You can unsubscribe anytime.

HD/HP-520-MS20

HARLEQUIN READER SERVICE—Here's how it works:

Accepting your 2 free books and 2 free gifts (gifts valued at approximately $10.00 retail) places you under no obligation to buy anything. You may keep the books and gifts and return the shipping statement marked "cancel." If you do not cancel, approximately one month later we'll send you more books from the series you have chosen, and bill you at our low, subscribers-only discount price. Harlequin Presents® Larger-Print books consist of 6 books each month and cost $5.80 each in the U.S. or $5.99 each in Canada, a savings of at least 11% off the cover price. Harlequin Desire® books consist of 6 books each month and cost just $4.55 each in the U.S. or $5.24 each in Canada, a savings of at least 13% off the cover price. It's quite a bargain! Shipping and handling is just 50¢ per book in the U.S. and $1.25 per book in Canada*. You may return any shipment at our expense and cancel at any time — or you may continue to receive monthly shipments at our low, subscribers-only discount price plus shipping and handling. *Terms and prices subject to change without notice. Prices do not include sales taxes which will be charged (if applicable) based on your state or country of residence. Canadian residents will be charged applicable taxes. Offer not valid in Quebec. Books received may not be as shown. All orders subject to approval. Credit or debit balances in a customer's account(s) may be offset by any other outstanding balance owed by or to the customer. Please allow 3 to 4 weeks for delivery. Offer available while quantities last.

▼ If offer card is missing write to: Harlequin Reader Service, P.O. Box 1341, Buffalo, NY 14240-8531 or visit www.ReaderService.com ▼

BUSINESS REPLY MAIL
FIRST-CLASS MAIL   PERMIT NO. 717   BUFFALO, NY

POSTAGE WILL BE PAID BY ADDRESSEE

HARLEQUIN READER SERVICE
PO BOX 1341
BUFFALO NY 14240-8571

NO POSTAGE
NECESSARY
IF MAILED
IN THE
UNITED STATES

to her and she needed to pull back. Sex was okay. This other stuff…*wasn't*.

"Um… I'm not sure. What did you have in mind?"

"There is a game on," he said.

"God, you are such a guy!"

"Yeah, I am," he acknowledged. "I thought you liked that."

She laughed. "I do."

"What do you usually do at night?"

"Listen to some music and sketch," she said, following him around the apartment.

"Let me go get changed and we can figure something out that's not art or sports… Do you want some sweats and T-shirt to wear?"

She nodded and followed him up to his bedroom. Brian had some art on the walls, and she saw a piece that she knew he'd bought from her gallery. "When did you get this?"

"A few months ago. You weren't in the gallery, but I didn't want to take a chance on someone else buying it."

"It's perfect in this space. I have another piece by this artist that I put in your large conference room. It has the same expansive feel as this landscape. But it's Santa Fe instead of Austin," she said.

"I can't wait to see it," he said. "You have a great eye for quality."

"I do," she acknowledged, realizing that she was looking at him. Brian was the kind of guy she wished she'd met in her twenties. But she hadn't. And they were from families that had a plethora of tension between them. And she needed to remember that she was here for his hot body and sexy kisses.

That was all.

Eight

Piper hadn't been sure what to expect as Brian's date to the Habitat for Humanity Boots and Boas charity gala.

The event was held at the Gaylord Texan Resort and Convention Center. Overlooking beautiful Lake Grapevine, the resort seemed to pay tribute to everything Texas. And it was bigger than most other places. The resort featured a water park and nightclubs along with accommodations and five-star amenities.

They had already started decorating for Christmas and Piper took her time walking through the lobby, admiring the festive decor. She was looking forward to the holidays this year, hoping that somehow her family would be cleared of all charges and maybe life would go back to normal.

Though, what *was* normal? She honestly didn't know anymore. After all, she was at this public event with a man—something she'd vowed to never do once her engagement had been broken—but Brian was changing her. This was the first event she'd attended in a long time where she wasn't stag. Something she refused to dwell too deeply on.

It was the kind of thing that she had enjoyed before everything had happened with the Wingate family, and she'd been painted with the same suspicions as her sister and nieces and nephews. But being on Brian's arm made her hardly even notice the stares and comments whispered behind hands.

Brian had bought them matching boots from Paul Bond, an American custom boot maker. She loved them. He'd gifted them to her the night before and she'd settled on a cocktail dress with a short skirt that ended above her knees to show off the boots. Brian hadn't been able to keep his hand off her thigh under the dinner table before the auction started, and that was nice too.

She'd always dreaded this gala because when she'd been twenty-four her fiancé had dumped her the night before this very event. It had been her first time donating a piece of art to auction off, and it had made that year's event sheer torture, but Ava had come with her and been her regal above-it-all self.

She'd saved Piper that year and that was something Piper hadn't forgotten.

There had been times when it was easy to focus on what a bitch her sister could be, but there was a very soft heart underneath the tough exterior. No one had even thought about saying anything to Piper, despite the rumors that were swirling that Ron had run off with another woman after dumping her.

They weren't really rumors, since that had been exactly what happened. But Ava had saved her. Now Brian was doing the same thing. Only this time he was protecting her from Ava and the scandal that surrounded the Wingate family. Many of the attendees were gossiping about alleged seizure of their property and their company, as well as investigations by the DEA, were pretty damning things, but Brian was her white knight. Keeping the louder gossips at bay and giving her a really fun evening when she hadn't expected one.

"Your sculpture is up next," Brian told her. "I'll let you know I'm going to go hard to get it for myself."

"You don't have to," she protested. "You being here has been more than enough."

"I'm not doing it to be nice. It will look perfect in the lobby of the building. I didn't like the piece you sent over and we have been discussing a mural which I think will make a nice backdrop to this," he said. "You said we needed something bold that speaks to our clients, and that sculpture definitely does. I mean, you captured the heart of what many of my younger clients are actually dealing with. I'm awed by your talent, Piper."

A flush of pride went through her and she smiled at him. "It's not really—"

"Don't do that," he said gruffly. "Take the compliment."

She nodded, and inwardly she thought about how she'd been raised and how it had once been more accepted to demur at kudos. But she had been in her studio day and night to produce this. It was a true labor of love in every sense of the word. "Thank you. I worked really hard at it. I had a recording of Xavier doing his spoken-word poetry that I played while I worked. His voice and word choices change as he moves between the two worlds. I just hope I captured enough of that."

She'd named the sculpture The Border and tried to show Xavier's struggle to stay on the right side of the law. The sculpture was one body but two faces looking in different directions. One contemplative, the other angry. In one hand was a notepad and pen, in the other, a gun.

"I'd say you did," Brian said, then glanced beyond her to where a couple of women were standing and watching them. "I think those ladies might agree."

She looked over her shoulder and noticed that the women were from a local PTA that she worked with to encourage arts. She waved them over. "Hi, Kim and Kathy. This is Brian Cooper. He's a family lawyer here in Dallas. Brian, these ladies are from the Thomas Hicks PTA. I work with them to bring an after-school art experience to the kids."

Everyone shook hands and Brian offered to brave the crowd at the bar and bring them back drinks. Everyone ordered a prosecco and he left.

"I love this piece," Kathy said. "I'm going to go back to our parents and see if we can get something like this for our school. Of course, a piece geared toward younger kids, but I think they all struggle with duality."

"I'd love to do a commission for you," Piper said. "Just let me know."

"We will. I have to warn you there have been some rumors about your family that a few concerned parents have raised with us," Kim informed her. "We know you, Piper, and have squelched them. But it might be hard to get this approved this school year."

Piper bit her lower lip to keep from saying something and then just smiled at the ladies. What could she say anyway? She couldn't change the opinions of the parents in the school district. Heck, she wasn't exactly sure what had happened at Wingate Enterprises, only knew that her family hadn't acted illegally. No one really seemed sure about who was responsible, though her nieces and nephews had a few leads that they were pursuing.

"There is no hurry for art," Piper said. "Will you two excuse me? I see someone I need to speak to."

"Of course," they said.

She walked away, trying not to dwell on the far-reaching aspects of the criminal activities of a company that she'd never had anything to do with. But that was easier said than done. Instead, she moved closer to the bar, where Brian stood, waiting his turn in line. He looked over at her, quirking one eyebrow.

Piper just forced a smile and indicated she'd be waiting in the corner. She was a social person by nature. But tonight, being in this room, she wanted to shrink into herself. To just blend in with the background until all the hurt that was buried under her skin disappeared.

"You okay?" Brian asked, coming over to her a few minutes later and handing her a champagne flute. She'd noticed he'd had a waiter deliver to the rest of their table.

"Yes. Just overwhelmed for a few moments," she admitted. "I want so much for everyone to see my sculpture for what it is and not filtered through the lens of the criminal activities that have engulfed Wingate Enterprises."

"I'm sure they will," he said.

But she knew that even Brian, who was a very forceful presence, couldn't change anyone's conceptions about herself and her family.

Brian went to a lot of these types of events and normally found them a bit dry and boring, but sitting next to Piper was eye-opening. She'd chilled out after the first prosecco, and since she'd been attending this event for close to fifteen years, she knew some random fact about nearly everyone in the room.

Her little asides had him in stiches as the gala progressed. She hadn't said anything, but it wasn't hard for him to guess that the Wingate scandal was having a profound effect on her life. He knew that her gallery wasn't seeing as much business due to that, and he wished there were some way he could help.

But investigations by the FBI and the DEA, and embezzling and drug dealing weren't necessarily in his wheelhouse. For tonight, though, he hoped he was providing enough of a distraction for Piper to enjoy herself and forget about all of that.

And for himself to forget, as well.

It was hard to be from two families who were at odds and just allow themselves to date. He knew that their rivalry over who to trust wasn't as bad here in Dallas, but when they were in Royal all of it would matter.

He still wasn't sure what her play was here. There were times when she let herself go and was the sensual woman he knew she could be. But other times he saw her barriers come up and she forced a wedge between them.

He knew that Ava had done that to his uncle Keith. Keith had been vocal when he'd spoken to Brian's dad about how he'd been blindsided by her refusing his calls after moving out of his house and into her own place in Royal.

Caution seemed to be more prudent where Piper was concerned but when she was naked in his bed was when he felt he saw the real woman. And playing it safe around her wasn't an option. Because every time he slept with her, he felt something change inside of him.

Fear was a funny thing. Brian used it sometimes to convince his clients to take action, and it motivated them to make the big decisions, but it could be crippling, as well. Right now, he was watching her laugh, her head thrown back in pure and utter delight. She turned to him and he felt a jolt of desire but also a punch right in the heart.

Could he trust her?

She tipped her head to the side. "Why are you watching me instead of the stage?"

"There isn't anything I want up there," he admitted.

She put her hand on him, her fingers caressing his inner thigh as she leaned forward. "But you want me?"

Her whispered words right in his ear made him hard in an instant. She brushed her fingertip over his erection and then wriggled her eyebrows at him. "As soon as my piece goes under the hammer, what do you say we head home?"

"Yes," he said, perhaps a little too forcefully as

several heads turned toward them. He just smiled at them and leaned over to whisper in Piper's ear all the filthy things he wanted to do to her.

The emcee announced her sculpture, *The Border*, and once it was brought onto the stage, they started the bidding. She pulled her hand from his leg and knotted hers together in her lap. Brian realized that she was nervous about this part and he couldn't blame her. He would be too. But he wanted her sculpture for his building and raised the bid. Someone on the other side of the room was keen to have it, as well, and kept bidding against him. Finally, Brian just made a huge increase and the room went silent.

"Any other bids?"

To his relief, he won the sculpture and there was a round of applause in the room. He looked over at Piper, who watched him with a look in her eyes that he couldn't read.

"Congratulations to you both," Mrs. Standard said from across the table. "That's a lovely piece and well worth every penny."

"Thank you," Piper said. "Will you excuse me?"

She grabbed her handbag and fled from the table.

"Thanks," Brian echoed. "I am going to go check on my lady."

He got up and followed Piper through the crowded ballroom. She was moving quickly and he had to lengthen his strides to keep up with her as she hurried down a long corridor and out onto one of the patios that were heated with lamps at this time of the year.

"Are you okay?" he asked.

She turned and her face was white, which amplified his concern for her.

"Piper?"

"Yes, I'm fine. I was…you bid a lot of money on my art," she said. "Why did you do that?"

"Because it's a really good piece and you created it. I want to see it every time I walk into my building. It might be based on the spoken-word poet, but I see you in it, Piper. The struggle you feel between being what society and Ava have wanted you to be and the goddess within."

The goddess within.

He saw things in her that no other man had seen before and that made her realize that things were getting too real. She wasn't ready for him. Or for anything like Brian in her life. They were truly all wrong for each other. She'd let this go on for too long because she was wildly attracted to him and had wanted to believe he wasn't the kind of guy to get serious with her.

But the emotions he stirred in her were strong and she wanted to believe—hell, she could see on his face that the feelings went both ways.

"I'm not a goddess," she said. "I'm just a woman

who is doing my best to get along. That's really all any of us can ask, right?"

He pulled her into his arms, the expression on his face so intense that she shivered. "Yes, it is. But there is more to you than that. You know it and I think you don't want me to know it. Why is that?"

She pulled away from him, shivering at the cold and yet at the same time hardening her emotions to what she had to do. She had to end this. On this night when she felt so many things. The highs and the lows of her life were centered now on this one man who'd come to mean more to her than she'd ever believed possible.

Which meant she had to cut him out of her life before he left her. There were a lot of barriers between them and they hadn't mattered as much earlier.

She had to do it now before…before he did it and it hurt so much more deeply. And, as selfish as it might be, *she* wanted to be the one to walk away so she could at least feel like she'd saved a bit of her soul.

"What you are seeing is age and maturity. I seem different than the other women you have dated because I have seen so much more of life," she said, channeling her inner Carrie Fisher and being that strong woman she knew she could be. "The truth is, when you are forty, I'll seem like everyone else."

He crossed his arms over his chest and tipped his head to the side as if he couldn't really comprehend what she was saying. "You want me to believe that everything that makes Piper Holloway so special is just age?"

When he put it like that, she admitted to herself, it sounded like an excuse. "You're being a little over-dramatic, but yes."

"Overdramatic?" he asked. "I'm pretty much known for being the coolest head in the room. I think you're trying to break up with me and I'm not even sure I know why. We aren't even serious per your design."

Piper sighed. This wasn't going well—she knew better than to start a conversation like this when she was so emotional. She liked Brian. Hell, she might even be starting to fall in love with him, but there was a part of her that knew she wasn't ready to be her true self with him. To expose the parts of herself that she ignored and hated. To give in to the passion that had always been her downfall.

It was as if part of her femininity was at stake and she didn't want to have to admit that to Brian, who was, in her eyes, the perfect male. He was everything she craved and nothing she would allow herself.

"I am breaking up with you," she said at last. "It's been fun but that is all it was meant to be."

"And I'm getting too real for you?" he asked roughly.

"Yes. I think about you a lot more than I should, Brian. And we both know there is no future in this…"

He cussed a blue streak and turned away from

her, his head bowed and his hands on his hips. The litany of curses eventually died down, but he stayed that way, with his back to her. And she knew she'd hurt him, which was the *last* thing she wanted, but now she could leave with her head held high and her heart battered but not totally broken.

He turned back around and the pain on his face brought tears to her eyes. She blinked quickly to keep them from falling.

"Why not? Is it because of the complicated history between my uncle and your sister?"

She swallowed hard. "Don't."

The one word was all she could muster. Her throat was tight as she tried to keep from crying while he was baring his soul to her. She struggled to keep hers hidden.

"Why not? I need the truth from you," he rasped. "Or is that something that you won't give me?"

"I'm not the woman you think I am," she said, thinking of how dangerous her unleashed passion could be. And she wasn't ready for this. Being here with him, having him buy a piece she'd made for such a large sum. He was focusing every eye on them and she didn't like who she was in the public spotlight.

"There is literally nothing you can say to convince me of that. I am not falling for an image of who I think Piper Holloway is. I'm falling for the artist who loses herself in her studio for days on end. Who painted a portrait of me that wasn't for show but showed the real man."

He came closer, held out his hand. "Won't you give us a chance?"

She bit her lip as tears did start falling, for she couldn't keep them back any longer. "I can't do this. This is a huge mistake. Goodbye, Brian."

She turned and forced herself to walk back into the hotel and out of his life.

Nine

The hour drive from Dallas to Royal gave her way too much time to think. A million times she'd thought of the other way things could have gone with Brian. But she didn't have time for regrets.

She'd made her choice and she had to live with it.

Besides, better to walk away now before she made a huge mistake. She liked to think that she had life sorted and could roll with the punches. Even if this one was harder to recover from.

Running back to Royal wasn't her style. She'd always prided herself on standing on her own, being able to find her place outside of her sister's shadow.

But when Ava called, sounding positively dreadful, Piper knew she couldn't turn her back on her.

The trip was long and uneventful. By rote she drove to the Wingate estate, which, of course, had been seized and was no longer Ava's home. Piper sat there in front of the mansion and the anger she felt toward Keith Cooper grew.

She knew that, at best, he'd taken advantage of her sister, but he'd been her sister and Trent's friend. He'd been a strong shoulder for Ava, though maybe he should have worked harder to help the family sort out the suspicious activities at Wingate. That would have really helped Ava.

It didn't help matters that she wanted to be angry at men with the surname of Cooper. She hated that Brian had pushed so hard and forced her hand. Made her have to admit that it was time to go back to her typical kind of guy. The kind who was divorced and already had a family or was still single because he hadn't even wanted one.

She put the car in gear and drove to the house that her sister had rented. Ava had been staying with Keith until her children's dislike of the way he tried to control her had finally gotten through to her. Piper took her weekender bag and went up the front steps.

Ava answered the door looking well put together and making Piper rethink the moto-style leggings and AC/DC T-shirt she wore under her leather biker jacket. Especially when her sister raised one eyebrow at her.

"It's not a mystery why you are still single," Ava said by way of greeting.

"They all have heard I'm your sister and are afraid to come too close," Piper said, deadpan.

Ava gave her a slight smile and hugged her. "Thank you for coming."

"You're welcome," Piper said. "I needed a break from Dallas anyway."

Ava led the way into the house and told Piper she could drop her bag in the study off to the left. She went to the eat-in kitchen and offered Piper something hot to drink. She shook her head. "I'm good. After that long drive, I could use a walk. Want to go for a stroll around the neighborhood?"

"Not really," Ava said. "But I will. Let me get changed."

Piper waited while her sister went and put on her Lululemons, donned a baseball cap and a pair of dark glasses, and declared herself ready. Piper wanted to poke fun at Ava for dressing as if the paparazzi were lurking behind her well-trimmed hedges, but she knew her sister had taken a beating over the last few months and kept her mouth shut.

The neighborhood was gated and Ava's privacy from the outside world was ensured, but the neighbors still talked about her. And while Piper knew her sister relished attention, she certainly did not want the kind she'd been subjected to lately.

"I hate this," Ava admitted. "I don't like not having a job to go to or being at odds with the kids. Nothing has been the same since Trent died."

Piper squeezed her sister's shoulder. This was exactly what she needed, someone else's problems to focus on to put her breakup with Brian into perspective. "It hasn't been. How could it be? You two were together so much that his death left a gaping hole in your life."

Ava nodded. "It did. I can only guess that's why I leaned so hard on Keith. I mean, as much as I want to say that he wasn't acting honorably, I have to admit he did comfort me."

"*Comfort* you? In what way?" Piper asked.

"Just as a companion. The trip to Europe did take my mind off my problems, and I let him handle things for me so I could just wallow in my grief and start to heal. He and Trent had been such good friends, especially when we were younger. It was nice to relive those memories and not have to worry about upsetting the kids by talking about their dad with them," Ava said. "But that was it."

Piper put her hand up. "That must have been nice. I don't know what I would have done in your situation."

"Count yourself lucky that you've never been in love and lost," Ava said.

Piper stopped walking. Ava knew about her broken engagement and the fact that she couldn't have kids. How could she say that Piper had never been in love? Sometimes Piper thought the fact that she'd been so in love had been the reason it had taken her so long to fall for a man again. To fall for Brian, who wasn't the right guy for her either, because he had dreams that she wouldn't deny him.

"What's wrong?"

Taken aback, she swallowed past the lump in her throat. "You know that I was in love," she said.

"Sorry, Piper, I thought we were talking about me. Could this just be about me for a few minutes?" Ava asked plaintively.

"When *isn't* it about you?" Piper retorted. She had driven all this way to keep her sister company and Ava was being…well, very Ava about it.

"Sorry. You're right," Ava said. "I just don't know what to do. I feel like I'm losing everyone important to me. The kids are distant and mistrust me because of Keith. And I'm snapping at you, which I know isn't fair."

Piper put her arm around her sister's waist and hugged her, and was gratified when Ava returned the embrace.

"I'll deny this if you repeat it, but I'm so lost."

"I am too," Piper admitted thickly.

They stood there for another moment, and for the first time Piper thought she really understood her sister. That they were both in the same spot and both connecting on a level she'd never expected.

"See? I can be supportive of someone else," Ava said wryly.

"I've always known that," Piper admitted. "You might not like the world to see it, but you care very deeply about your friends and family."

"That's right. I think that's what got me into the mess with Keith. I was just so lonely when Trent died," Ava confessed.

"It happens to everyone. But you're on the right path now," Piper said warmly.

She wished she could say more. Talk to Ava about Brian and everything that was going on right now, but this bond felt so new and Piper suspected it might be fragile if she mentioned a Cooper. The rivalry between their families was real even though when she'd been with Brian she'd never dwelled on it.

Brian was in court and needed to be on his A game, but instead he kept rerunning the night of the charity gala to figure out what he'd done or said to set Piper off. He knew that her emotions had been running high due to people talking about her and the Wingates, and he completely empathized with her for feeling that way. He would probably have gotten drunk and started a fight…except that wasn't his way.

He wished sometimes that he *was* that kind of

guy. The kind who just felt things for a moment, expressed them and then moved on, but he never had been. He knew he was ruled by intellect and not passion—normally. Piper hadn't been wrong in any of the things she'd said the other night except when she'd been talking about him.

She didn't know him at all if she thought he'd be influenced by age. That he couldn't see the woman she was. What was he missing? Something he had said must have convinced her he didn't want her long-term.

"All rise," the bailiff said, and Brian stood, making sure his client did, as well. He knew he had to push his thoughts of Piper to the back of his mind until they were done in court.

He charged a respectable rate and his client deserved his full attention. So he did his job, ensuring his client was awarded as much monetarily from the breakdown of her marriage as she was entitled to. He also helped her get the custody agreement she wanted and tried to negotiate her desired move out of her neighborhood, but her husband wasn't about to budge on that front. The judge suggested that they either accept each other's terms or go to mediation, which they'd done three times already. Finally, thinking of Piper and the fact that she'd summarily ended their relationship, he turned to his client during the recess.

"Do you think you'll want to move?"

"No. My kids love that house and it's their home. I just hate that he won't let me," she said.

"We can go back to mediation or we can let him think he's won this and ask for more money," he told her. "I think I can get more for you if you have to stay in that house. At least the HOA fees."

"Sure. I don't want him to think he's won," Karen said. "God, I sound so petty, don't I?"

"You sound like someone who is dealing with a complex breakup. Everyone is petty when that happens."

"Thanks," she murmured. "But surely that's not the case with you."

"Me more than most," he admitted. But the truth was, he didn't want to hurt Piper; he wanted her back. But first, he needed to figure out what he'd missed.

"I doubt that, Brian. You've been so fair the entire time. That's the thing about this. I didn't want a divorce. I liked our life. He's the one who cheated and made it clear he won't stop. I think I want to hurt him because he didn't like our life."

"There's nothing wrong with that. But I don't have to tell you that the law doesn't work like that," he said gently.

"No, you don't. I just wish it did." She sighed. "Okay, see if you can get more money and I want a stipulation that if he moves out of the county, I can move wherever I want."

"I will see what I can do," he said, gathering his notes to go and talk to the other lawyer.

Forty minutes later they had more money and the proviso that Karen had asked for, and he looked at the couple as they both stood in the courtroom. The animosity was gone. There was nothing left to argue about and they both seemed to know it. Brian decided right then that he definitely preferred what had happened between himself and Piper to this. He vowed that if he got married, he'd never end up here. But, of course, Karen hadn't expected to end up in divorce court either.

So was that why Piper was reluctant to take things to the next level? He hadn't been talking about marriage or anything like that. He'd simply wanted to date. Yet, at the same time, it felt like there was more between them than just sex. But maybe he'd been wrong. Did it stem from watching Ava allow his uncle Keith to protect her and help her out? And what had really gone on between those two?

He reached out to Keith via text and asked if he had time to talk, then headed back to his office. The statue Brian had won at Boots and Boas had been delivered and his assistant had overseen its placement in the center of the lobby. Brian stopped and looked at it. Saw the pain and the yearning and truth in the expression on the figure in the sculpture and knew he had to do whatever he could to get Piper back into his life.

He called her number instead of texting to see if she'd answer. The call went to voice mail, but he got a text a moment later from her.

Piper: I am not ready to talk.

He thought of a million different responses but none of them felt right, so he took a picture of the sculpture and sent it to her.

Brian: You're brilliant.

He pocketed his phone and walked away from the statue, pretending that seeing it didn't cause a cascade of feelings that he didn't want to have, but did anyway. Because the woman who had crafted it, the woman who'd seen so deeply into the fact that Xavier was two different men, hadn't trusted him enough to show him hers.

Spending time with her nieces always made Piper feel better. She'd been keeping Ava company when Harley and Beth had called to see if she wanted to join them for pedicures. It didn't escape her attention, however, that they had waited until Ava was at a meeting with her lawyer before extending the invite. She understood it, yet at the same time wished there was some way she could fix this for them all.

"What color are you thinking?" Harley asked. The youngest of her sister's two daughters had medium-brown hair that she wore long and straight. She had green eyes and an easy smile. She was a very natural and earthy girl.

"I was thinking something midnight blue," Piper replied. Brian's eyes were dark and black, but there were times when she caught the slightest hint of blue in them.

"I like it. I was thinking something in either red or maybe a festive autumn color," Harley said.

"Like orange?" Beth teased her. Her eldest niece had dark blond hair and always had highlights in it. She was tall and sophisticated.

"All I can see now is something pumpkin colored," Harley said.

Piper smiled at her niece. "You should have brought Daniel…he has a good eye for color."

"I would have, but he and Grant are having a little daddy-son time," Harley informed her. "As well as packing up. The move to Thailand is taking a lot of hard work. We have to decide what to keep and what to store. We have a shipping container and movers coming to get it all arranged, but I honestly feel like I'm never going to get it all finished."

"I'm glad you took the time to come today. You definitely can use a break," Beth said.

"Me too. Seeing you and Grant married makes me so happy. You are perfect for each other," Piper chimed in. "I mean, you've been through a lot together and clearly are on the same page."

"Are you not on the same page with someone?" Harley asked as they all took their bottles of nail polish and were led to the pedicure chairs.

"Not exactly. It's just that it's hard to be on the same page when you are so wildly different from each other." Piper sighed pensively. "But I have tried…"

"Who are we talking about?" Beth demanded. "I didn't realize you were dating anyone. Although I did see you with Brian Cooper at Harley's wedding."

"I was dating him," Piper admitted. "We called it quits before I came back to Royal."

"Why? Is he like Keith? If so, it's good that you kicked him to the curb." Beth's tone sharpened. "Keith had so much influence over Mom, he was changing her. And not for the better."

"Was he? It's hard to think of our mother letting anyone have that much influence over her," Harley mused.

"He did," Piper said. "It was hard to talk to her about it because she was so defensive."

"Definitely," Beth agreed. "But what's the deal with Brian?"

"He's not like Keith," Piper said. In fact, he was nothing like any other man she'd met. He seemed to get her and to understand that she wasn't marching to the same drum as everyone else.

"So what's the problem then?" Harley interjected.

"He's eleven years younger than me."

"So? I know you don't care about that," Beth retorted. "What's this *really* about?"

Piper looked at her nieces and fought to find the

strength to tell them. She'd always felt so much an outsider in her own family but right now she could use someone to talk to. Someone who would understand where she was coming from. Beth was nine years younger than she was and Harley was 17 years younger so she hadn't shared much of her broken engagement with them. They'd been so young at the time. "You're right, it's not the age difference. It's a lot more to do with my baggage. I've had a really bad breakup once before, and I promised myself I wouldn't go through that again."

"But why end things with Brian?" Harley asked, confused.

"He's Keith's nephew, for one. Your mom isn't going to be a huge fan of me dating him."

"Like you care what Mom says," Beth quipped.

"I do. I mean, she can be overbearing at times, but I don't want to ever hurt her," Piper admitted.

"If you like him, Mom will understand," Beth said.

Did she like him? Of course she did. That's why she broke things off with him. And another reason why she'd come home to Royal.

She remembered the way he'd hired her to decorate his building and then left her alone to curate the pieces that she'd use. He was a man who hired experts and then stepped back and let them run with it.

Maybe that was why it had been so hard to leave Dallas the night of the gala. She hadn't wanted to leave him. Truth was, she liked *so many* things about him. But he was young and eventually he was going to bring up kids and she couldn't have them. Didn't want to have to admit that to him. So she'd left before she had to.

"He sounds great, Piper," Harley murmured. "But you haven't answered my earlier question. What's really going on?"

"I don't know how to put it into words," she said at last. "It's just not going to work out."

"Well, I'm sorry to hear that." Beth sighed. "Sounds like he was making your happy for a little while."

"I'm sorry too," Harley said. "But there is more to relationships than just making someone happy."

Her nieces were very smart, and she felt so lucky to have them in her life. Piper changed the subject to Thanksgiving and how nice it was to have Harley back this year. She let the conversation drift around her and when she left her nieces to head back to Ava's she realized she needed to do this more. Talking to them had made her realize that there were other complications in life than just her own fears.

Was it her fear that was holding her back? Or was she justified to feel that Brian might cause her to forget all the safety measures she'd put in place? Her life worked because she kept that wild, passionate side of hers hidden away. Letting it out wasn't something she was sure she could do.

It gave her something to think about as she drove home past the Texas Cattleman's Club where all of the Wingates had been members for as long as Piper could remember—well, the women hadn't been admitted until the early 2000s—but she knew that her family no longer felt welcome at the club since their assets had been seized and their home put into foreclosure.

As hard as it was to face gossip in Dallas, at least she'd been removed from this sort of day-to-day thing. She wasn't sure how she could handle that. Stopping at an intersection, she had an epiphany of sorts while waiting for the light to turn green. She realized she was trying to distract herself from the fact that she still missed Brian.

Piper sighed. It would be nice if parting ways with a man meant that she stopped thinking and caring about him. She knew that her actions were going to be for the best in the long run, but right now she ached. For, despite everything, she couldn't stop yearning for him…which made her feel like a soppy young woman instead of the wise goddess she was trying so hard to be.

But she just shook her head and felt the weight of her gold orb earrings brushing against her neck. She knew that no matter what she wanted to project, inside she was still that twenty-four-year-old with a broken engagement when she thought about forever with any man. Her relationships after Ron and before Brian had all ended by her own hand.

Maybe it was time to stop trying to keep from being hurt again by ending things with Brian until he found the broken thing inside of her that had made Ron leave? But if she did that she'd have to put her heart on the line and she wasn't sure she had the strength to do that. Being a goddess and standing on her own above everyone else was one thing but trusting Brian not to hurt her…that was something bigger. At Harley's reception she'd wanted to have a partner, but she realized now she'd gotten more than she'd bargained for with Brian.

Ten

Piper had typed a text to Brian just to chat and deleted it about eighty-five times. She missed him, but she knew that she should just leave it be. So why couldn't she? Added to the fact that he was Keith's nephew, she knew that it should be enough to convince her to stop thinking about him, but she hadn't.

She'd even woken up in the middle of the night, her body craving his. Only to be filled with dismay to find the empty space next to her. Given that they'd only slept together a handful of times, her intense longing for him wasn't rational. But then, she knew that matters of the heart rarely were.

She was going to have find her way through this.

However she did it, whatever that meant, she had to stay strong and be that wise goddess she wished she were. She didn't feel wise at all today as she watched her sister slowly lose her sparkle as more pieces of Trent's legacy were taken away from her and her children. Her confidence had taken a hit when Trent died, but losing the house and having the company seized was like a knife to Ava. And Piper saw her put on her old attitude when the kids were around or she thought she needed to keep up the pretense, but honestly there were moments when her sister seemed truly lost.

Piper poured them both a glass of wine and went to find Ava sitting in front of the fireplace. There was a nice blaze going and it heated the room. She looked up at the space above the mantel where Ava had always had a portrait of herself and Trent and the kids in her home. It must kill her sister to sit here in a rented house on rented furniture in a place that wasn't home, unsure that she'd ever get back into her own home.

"It's wine o'clock," Piper said to announce herself.

"Thank goodness," Ava said.

Piper handed her sister one of the glasses. "To sisters."

"Sisters," Ava murmured, clinking her glass against Piper's. "Oh, Pip, what am I going to do?"

Piper curled her legs underneath her as she sat down next to her sister on the sofa. "You're going to remember you are Ava Wingate. You raised some great kids and helped build Wingate Enterprises into the success it was. Your family has taken a hit but you're not out of the game."

Ava tipped her head to the side as she took a sip of the wine. "I am that woman, but I'm also the one who was so scared to be alone that I fell into Keith's arms and let him make decisions for me. I just… I just went along with it. That's not me."

"I know," Piper said.

"The kids don't. Harley didn't really even want me at the wedding. I think they blame me for everything," Ava said. "I'm so mad at Trent for dying and leaving me. I know it's not his fault and that makes no sense, but I miss him, and I needed him. He promised me seventy-five years of marriage."

Piper blinked to keep from letting her tears fall. "You know if there was any way in hell that he could have delivered on that promise, he would have. He thought you hung the moon."

Ava let her head drop to the back of the sofa and Piper heard the ragged sound of her breathing. "Sometimes I feel like the real me died the same day he did. And some imposter has been trying to act like me."

Piper scooted closer to Ava, putting her wineglass on the coffee table and pulling her sister into her arms. Ava had never been one to show any cracks in her life and this had to be hard for her. The woman who always used her iron will to make things happen and ensure that her family was safe, was now helpless to keep it from crumbling.

"You did the best you could. I know this will shock you, but you're not superwoman, Ava."

Her sister started laughing and pulled back to punch her playfully in the shoulder. "I know that."

"I think you forget it sometimes. Cut yourself some slack. Keith came to you as a friend and you took him at face value. It's not your fault that you couldn't reciprocate his feelings. After Ron reneged on our engagement, I thought I was cool, but after my next few relationships ended, I realized that I couldn't trust a man. *Any man.* Ron had taken that from me. I still struggle with that."

"I know you do. Are you seeing anyone?" Ava asked, wiping her eyes with a tissue.

"I have been. But I broke it off," Piper said.

"Why?"

"He makes me feel reckless…not like the woman I need to be. He's also younger than me."

Ava turned to face her. "Why does that matter?"

"It doesn't. I mean, I know it doesn't, but it is just one more thing."

"So far those obstacles aren't insurmountable," Ava said. "One of us should be in a healthy relationship."

Talking to Ava had made Piper realize that maybe she should give Brian another chance. That long-ago hurt was keeping her from happiness. She wanted to think she was beyond it, but she knew she wasn't. And maybe it was time she made up her mind to let it go. To trust another man.

"Actually, you know him."

"I do?" she asked. "Who is he?"

"Brian Cooper."

Her sister's jaw dropped open. "Keith's *nephew*?"

"Yes," she said.

"I wouldn't have thought of him and you together," Ava said.

"But you just—" Why did she think that her sister had changed?

"You're right. You're smart, Pip. You are never going to let a man walk all over you like I did with Keith."

Piper had spent the afternoon at the high school in Royal, talking to the art students. She remembered her own time in these halls, which had changed a lot since she'd graduated. Yet there was something so familiar about it. Especially the art room with the smell of acrylic paints and clay. For the first time since she'd left Dallas, she felt like she could breathe. She took a deep inhalation and closed her eyes.

Cheri, the art teacher, was a friend of Piper's, but she'd been surprised when Cheri had invited her to come in and view her students' work and talk to them about career options in the art world. Some of the students were really talented and Piper had made the offer to showcase some of them in her student exhibit in the summer. The teacher had smiled at the idea.

"I'm going to frame it as a gallery in Dallas. Right now, this town is pretty much anti-Wingate," Cheri said, "and although I know you don't have anything to do with the business, some of the parents might not see it that way. This offer isn't something the students should miss because of that."

"Thanks, Cheri," Piper said. She left but felt edgy and ticked off. She hated small-mindedness, and of course she didn't want anyone to think she condoned breaking the law, but her family was innocent.

She had her head down as she walked up Main Street, not really paying attention to where she was going, and bumped into someone. Glancing up to apologize, she stopped in her tracks.

It was Brian.

"You okay?"

She shook her head. "Yeah, thanks. Sorry for bumping into you."

"Don't worry about that. But you look pissed as hell."

"I am," she admitted. "I just came from the high school where I was told in a very nice way that some parents might not want their kids' art to hang in my gallery. I mean, give me a freaking break!"

"That's not fair to the kids or you," he said. "You're not part of Wingate Enterprises."

"No, I'm not. But I am part of the family." She sighed. "I've been dealing with this to a lesser extent in Dallas. Anyway, that doesn't matter. What are you doing here?"

He tipped his head to the side, studying her. "I was hoping to see you. Want to have dinner so we can talk about things?"

Did she? Yes. But the things she'd have to talk about…she didn't want to. She had made a break and she knew if she took a step back toward him it would be harder to leave again. "I can't."

Brian clenched his jaw but then relaxed it into a smile and she realized that he wasn't happy about their breakup, but he was being a gentleman. Wasn't that everything she adored about him? He was *always* a decent guy. The kind of man who deserved everything that life had to offer. A successful career, a sophisticated woman by his side…and kids.

A house full of them if he so chose.

"Fine. But hiding with your family isn't going to last forever," he reminded her.

"I'm not hiding. I'm here to help support Ava. It's a rough time for her," she said. "She's still trying to get over Keith."

"How do you figure? Ava's not a shrinking violet," he said. "And she broke up with him."

"Why was she not herself when she was living with Keith?" Piper asked, realizing she was letting this devolve into a fight. She wanted to fight. Wanted to yell at him because it would make her feel better about the fact that they weren't together.

But she wasn't going to do that. "I'm sorry. It was nice seeing you."

She walked away and didn't look back. Just got to her car and drove out of town, hoping that it would be as easy to get over Brian as it had been to drive away.

Piper wasn't prepared to see Brian when he showed up at Ava's door later that evening. She and her sister had made tacos for dinner and spent the evening laughing and talking about men. It had been nice to talk to Ava and feel her sister had her back.

For so many years she'd felt like she was on the outside of the family looking in, trying to be someone she wasn't. Brian had offered her a chance to be herself. But dare she trust herself enough to give in to her passionate side and live her life? Or was she always going to be afraid of it?

But here he was on her sister's doorstep, stubble on his jaw, and he looked tired. Like he hadn't been sleeping well. He clearly wasn't about to let her close him out as he stood there. "Sorry to show up like this, but I just didn't want to do this by text."

"That's okay. Um, let me grab my coat and we can go for a walk. This is Ava's home and I don't know—"

"Who is it?" Ava called as she came down the hallway.

"Brian," Piper told her.

"Hello, Ava," Brian said. "I'm sorry to show up unannounced but I need a word with Piper."

Ava gave him a hard look and then shook her head and forced a smile. "You can use the study."

Ava turned and walked away from them both. Piper stepped back to allow Brian to enter the foyer. She gestured to the left where the study was. As soon as he entered, she followed him, closing the door behind them. He moved farther into the room and took a seat on the leather settee while she stood there with her back against the hardwood door, trying to get herself under control.

Now that he was here, she discovered she'd missed him so much more than she'd even realized. And yeah, he looked exhausted, but also so good to her eyes. She was drinking him in as if it had been years since she had seen him instead of days. His voice was a low rumble as he talked, and she realized how much she'd missed the cadence of it. He leaned back, spread his arms along the back of the settee and just stared at her.

"What did you say?"

"I asked if you were going to sit down so we could talk," he said. "Are you feeling okay?"

No.

She was a big hot mess, and spending time with her sister who was in the same boat hadn't really helped her at all. Piper only hoped that he couldn't see it. She forced a smile. "Of course."

She sat down in one of the armchairs, perching on the edge before realizing what she was doing and sitting back, hopefully to give the illusion that she was chill with this. "What brings you here?"

"Are you serious?" he asked. There was an intensity in him that she hadn't noticed before. She had the feeling she was seeing his courtroom persona, and honestly, he was rather intimidating.

"Yes. I thought we said everything we needed to the other day." Piper crossed her legs and wrapped her arms around herself.

"No, we didn't. I had hoped that once we had some time apart, you'd realize that," he bit out.

"Realize what?"

"That what we have is too good to give up on," he said. "If you don't want to move to the next level that's fine with me. I'm willing to keep things fun and light."

She shook her head. "One of the things I have admired about you is that you don't lie. Please don't start now."

"Fine. I don't want to be casual. Do you think I like feeling like this?" he asked.

"No," she admitted. This was hard and not anything she was prepared to deal with. "How about if we just leave things until after Thanksgiving, and then when we are both back in Dallas we can—"

"No, Piper, I don't want to leave this. I want to fix this. I'm still not sure what your objection to the two of us is," he said. "The age thing is a nonissue, so please don't bring it up again."

"It's more than that. You have a young man's dreams and I don't—"

"Stop." He cut her off as he got to his feet. "You are being closed-minded."

"Better than being ignorant," Piper retorted, standing, as well.

"We both know I'm not," he said. "If you're going to insult me, you'll have to work a bit harder."

"I don't have to do anything. I'm a grown-ass woman and if I decide to end things with you, that's it."

"God dammit, Piper Holloway, you are ticking me off!" he said.

"Good. Maybe you'll understand that I'm saying we are over."

"Is this what you do with all your relationships? End them before they begin?" he demanded.

His words hit a little too close to home and she hated that he'd pegged her so easily. "I don't think that's any of your business."

He tipped his head to the side and strode closer to her, leaving a few inches between them, but she knew it was his own self-control that kept him there and not in her face. God, she wanted to throw herself into his arms and kiss the hell out of him. There was no one quite like this man, she realized. But she also knew she wasn't thinking clearly. Her emotions were out of control, roiling through her like a tornado, and while she was sorely tempted to give in to them, she didn't want to destroy herself and Brian in the process.

"It *is* my business, Piper. I wanted everything with you and you are too stuck in the past to see it."

"I'm not. We just aren't as compatible as you want us to be," she said to reinforce her point.

"Fine. Fuck it. I'm leaving," he snapped, brushing past her and stalking to the door, but when he got there, he stopped.

He was leaving.

That was when it hit her—she loved him. She felt it all the way to her bones. It hurt so much to watch him turning his back on her and walking out. But that was okay. It was better this way.

But it didn't feel better. It felt so bittersweet.

"You know what I think?" he demanded, turning to face her.

She really didn't want to know. Because she was teetering on the edge, on the verge of losing it completely. So, out of sheer desperation, she gathered all the steely emotional armor she'd built over the years around her.

"Please enlighten me," she said, trying not to wrap her arms around herself again.

"You can't let yourself love any man. I don't know

if it's a control thing or what, but I'm beginning to realize why you are still all alone."

"You don't know jack shit," she said, losing her temper. "I'm not alone. I have my family and my art."

"Your family is a mess. I'd think you'd want one of your own."

"Don't you dare say anything about my family when your uncle is the cause of what has made my sister ignore the business for so long. I won't take the risk of losing myself in a man. That's when mistakes happen, big mistakes. And I can't have a family of my own. I'm barren. See yourself out," she said, brushing past him and heading up the stairs to her room.

She hated that he'd driven her to lose her temper, but it was better for him to hear it all so he'd realize there was no hope of reconciliation for them.

He wanted to go after her but when a woman walked away in the home where she was staying, he knew better than to follow. He glanced to the end of the hallway, saw Ava standing there. She didn't say a word, but he felt her censure.

"She doesn't know me at all if she thinks that I give a damn about her reproductive abilities," he said, then he turned and walked out of the house, getting into his car and driving faster than the speed limit down the road toward the front of the gated community.

He slammed on the brakes when he noticed people

walking on the sidewalk with fishing poles. Damn. She was making him stupid and reckless.

Hell, she hadn't made him anything. Love had. In his mind, the rant he wanted to have at her ran on an endless loop. When had he said that he wanted only biological children? When had he said that he wanted her to choose him over her family?

What kind of man did she think he was? Had she even tried to get to know him? He knew the answer had to be no. If she had, she wouldn't have made such blind and wrong assumptions about him and what was important to him.

He pushed those thoughts aside and drove to the house he kept in Royal. His uncle had been texting him to get together since it was close to Thanksgiving, but given that Brian had been dating Piper, he had thought it best to stay away.

But now…hell, did it really matter if he had dinner with Uncle Keith? It didn't matter that the Wingates all suspected Keith of somehow being responsible for their trouble. They had no proof, and as he'd just witnessed in Piper's irrational diatribe against him, they weren't above jumping to completely false conclusions.

In no mood to go home and be alone, he stopped at the Texas Cattleman's Club. He knew he needed to get drunk. But getting sloshed alone was never a good idea. If he did, he'd probably give in to the temptation to drive back over to Ava's rented house, lie to the guard again and stand outside in the yard doing something asinine like yelling her name or playing the song that had been playing the first time he held her in his arms.

He wasn't going to let that happen.

He had pride.

Sober, at least, he had pride. The drunk version of him had always leaned more into his emotions than his rational side. And he knew better than to go back to Piper. She had made herself clear twice now. How many times did he need to hear a woman tell him she didn't want him before it sank in?

He saw some friends who were about his age that he'd known while growing up and joined them. They were drinking whiskey and talking about the Cowboys, and it was just what Brian thought he needed until he remembered that Piper had agreed to come with him to Thanksgiving at his folks' house and then the Dallas Cowboys game.

"Dude, you okay?"

"Yeah, why?" Brian asked.

"You're staring at that whiskey like you are planning to throw it against the wall," Leon said.

"Just had a bad breakup," Brian admitted.

"Well, hell, boy, why didn't you say? We should have ordered tequila," Leon said.

"No one wants to admit he got kicked to the curb by a woman," Brian grumbled, downing his whiskey in one long swallow and signaling the waiter for another one. "And tequila on a weeknight is never a good idea."

"I know that. But my old lady is in College Station with her sorority sisters and I've got nothing to go home to," Leon said.

"Me either. That's what I've been trying to fix. How'd you and Viv get together?" Brian asked. "I always thought I had some kind of game, but recently it seems as if I have nothing."

Leon played with the whiskey glass, rolling it between his palms before taking a sip. "We got together after graduation. I came back to take over the ranch and she took one look at me in the diner one day and said, 'You want to ask me out.'"

Brian laughed. That sounded like Vivian. She'd always been ballsy and unafraid to go after what she wanted. "And you were smart enough to do it."

"Damn straight. A woman like Viv doesn't come along twice in a lifetime," Leon said. "Tell me about your gal. I'm guessing you want her back?"

"I do," Brian said, taking another swallow of the whiskey. He did want her back. No matter how many times she pushed him away, he still couldn't stay away from her. But a man had his pride. He couldn't keep going back, could he? "She's, um, Piper Holloway. You know her?"

"I know of her. Dang boy, she's pretty sophisticated and out of your league."

"I'm a high-paid, highly respected lawyer, Leon. I've got some polish," Brian reminded his friend.

"I know, but Piper has something else. She just seems more metropolitan. But as you pointed out, so are you. So it's not that. What is it that's keeping you two apart?"

It was on the tip of his tongue to tell him what she'd said but he knew better than to share that with another living soul. She'd claimed she was afraid to lose herself in him. But why? Had he been too forceful, too domineering? And how could she lose herself in him when she'd been hiding her true self from the world?

"She says we are too different, that we want different things from life," he said at last.

"And all you want is one with her," Leon murmured.

"Exactly. I'm fucked," Brian said.

Eleven

Ava was gone when Piper woke up in the morning and she contemplated going back to Dallas. Her sister was going to be okay and Piper had realized overnight that she would be too, eventually. What had always worked in the past when she'd ended a relationship was to pour herself back into her art.

She had a commission for a client in New York who missed Texas and wanted something that reminded her of her home state. Piper pulled out her sketchbook, but her mind was empty. No matter how she tried to come at the work, she couldn't think of anything. So she just started sketching because sometimes moving her pencil over the paper sparked ideas. She liked the sound of the scratching and started simply, with just a face. Then, over time, she made the jaw a little bit stronger before drawing crossed lines to place the eyes and the nose.

The eyes she drew were wide-set and the nose a sharp blade that reminded her very much of Brian's. She pushed that thought aside, let go of her conscious thoughts and just sketched. It wasn't long until the image took shape, and more than the nose looked like Brian. It *was* Brian.

She'd drawn him as he'd looked when she told him she couldn't have kids. And it would be easy to tell herself that the look on his face had been disgust, but it had been a shock and, of course, being Brian, empathetic, as well. He'd been ticked at her, but more because she'd misjudged him.

Tossing the sketchbook aside, she stood up to pace to the window that looked over the backyard. She saw that her sister hadn't left the property but was sitting on a bench in the backyard. By herself.

This was it, she thought. This was what the Holloway women had come to. Two lonely women who had lost on love. Ava when Trent died and when she'd trusted the wrong man, and Piper…well, she'd lost because after Ron she'd never been able to trust *any* man. She'd never let herself love again because she was afraid to be hurt again.

This time, though, she was pretty damn sure she'd hurt Brian. Badly. She could justify it ten ways to

Sunday and tell herself that he'd get over it—get over *her*—and find someone closer to his own age. But would she?

Could she move on from pushing away the only man she'd fallen in love with? She knew better than to believe that it would be easy. But Brian was gone. There was no way he'd come back after what she'd said to him, and really, how could she rebuild his broken trust when hers was still tattered and in pieces?

She'd have to let down her guard, really just start being herself and be comfortable in her own skin. Was that even possible? She wasn't too sure.

Piper could only feel safe thinking about trusting him because he had left and that had been final. She sank to the floor and drew her knees up to her chest, resting her forehead on them. *This*. This was why she wasn't the wise goddess she projected at the gallery. She was still broken from something that had happened in her twenties, and like someone who hadn't had their wound properly attended to, she had learned to live with that fractured part of herself.

And while she had pretended that being broken didn't really matter, and that she was fine, deep down she wasn't. She hadn't been since her engagement had ended…until Brian danced with her at Harley and Grant's reception. He'd swept her off her feet, starting a cascade of change inside of her, but she'd just kept putting rocks back in the dam to keep it in place. And she'd succeeded in driving him away.

This time for good.

She was safe. No one could hurt her. Alone. *Again.* By her own design.

"Ugh!" she yelled, getting up from the floor.

She was making herself angry with all the whining she was doing mentally. If she wanted Brian back in her life then, by God, she'd get him. If that meant convincing him that she'd made a mistake—admittedly that was going to be the hardest part, but she could do it.

He was worth it.

Wasn't he?

Ava had pointed out that Brian wasn't Keith any more than Ava and Piper were the same. He was a good man who'd worked hard all of his life and he was kind and funny. Sexy as hell.

She'd never find another man like him again, she thought.

Never.

That had to be enough to get her out the door. Piper turned and saw her reflection in the mirror. She looked as if she hadn't had a shower in days, and the fine lines she'd been trying to hide with retinol were visible this morning. She looked like a woman who'd given up.

A woman who'd forgotten who she was. She *was*

that wise goddess. Piper knew it. She'd worked hard to get where she was in life and to surround herself with good friends and family she loved very much.

There was no reason Brian couldn't be a part of that. She had to deal with any lingering doubts that Ava and the rest of the family had, but then she was going to find a way to try again with Brian.

She winked at herself in the mirror. Feeling loads better now that she'd decided on action. Action was better than wallowing any day.

She showered and put on makeup and her favorite outfit of skinny jeans and a funky sweater before going to find Ava. Her sister was on the phone and that was fine with Piper. She had already made her peace with her choice and she had the insight that only people who were unsure had to rush.

Once you were solid in the knowledge of what you wanted, time didn't matter. She would take as long as she had to in order to win Brian back.

Uncle Keith was in an odd mood when Brian arrived for dinner. But he was glad to see him. The big house was empty except for this housekeeper who'd served dinner, but then she left too. Keith poured them both a Jack and Coke pretty hard throughout the meal.

"I didn't think you'd be back in Royal until December," Uncle Keith said after they'd retired to his study to watch ESPN.

It seemed to Brian that they'd made the move so that his uncle could be closer to the whiskey, and he wondered if losing Ava was still an open wound for Keith the way losing Piper as for Brian.

He poured them both another Jack and Coke, and took a seat across from his uncle. The room was dark and masculine, smelling of cigars and pine. There were stacks of paper on the desk and the large-screen TV dominated one wall while floor-to-ceiling book-cases occupied the other.

"I followed Piper, hoping…" Brian trailed off. Truthfully, he didn't really want to get into it again. He was turning into a sad sack, first with Leon and now with his uncle.

"Piper Holloway?"

"Yes, sir," Brian said, leaning back and propping his ankle on his knee. "We had been dating, but she ended things abruptly."

"She dumped you?" Uncle Keith asked incredu-lously.

"Yeah," Brian admitted. "She's so unsure of me. She's afraid she'll lose herself if she's with me."

"Really? She never really struck me as the force-ful kind," Keith said.

"Oh, there is a lot more to Piper than most people see," Brian said. That was probably why he'd been so convinced that what they had was special. She'd let him in, and had looked past his barriers and seen the real him, as well.

"Same with Ava. Everyone sees her as a force to be reckoned with, and she is, but after Trent got so sick, she just couldn't hold it together any longer," Keith said.

"That had to be hard for you to see. Losing your best friend and then seeing his widow at the breaking point—I would have been wanted to step in and fix things too," Brian said.

"Damn, boy, we have more in common than I would have guessed. I did the best I could. I love her," Keith said gruffly. "I just wanted to take care of her."

"If she's anything like Piper, she probably wanted to do it on her own."

"Yeah. Just like college," Keith said, getting up to pour himself another drink.

"I thought y'all were just friends in college. Was it more?"

"I wanted it to be, but Trent cut me out. He had more money back then and didn't hesitate to splash it around. Ava soon started spending more time with him," Keith told him, his voice heavy with emotion.

"That must have been hard, but you were young and moved on," Brian reminded him. "I know you had some good times with the women you married."

Keith turned around, his eyes bloodshot and his steps a little unsteady as he made his way back to his armchair, bringing the bottle of Jack Daniels with him. "That I did, but none of those women were Ava."

Had his uncle been pining for Ava Holloway Wingate all those years? That didn't seem like the kind of man that Keith Cooper was. But emotions were something that most men in their family didn't like to talk about.

"Then Trent got sick and she needed me," he said, almost to himself.

"That was a tragedy. I know you were there for them both through the illness," Brian added.

"Least I could do."

"I would do the same for Piper," he said. Would he? He wasn't sure he'd be able to be friends with Piper if she married another man. He'd eventually drift out of her life. But Keith hadn't been able to get that distance.

"I know you would, son."

"So what really happened between you and Ava?" Brian asked. "I thought you two were getting really close."

"We were," he said. "But once we were back from Europe…no one can compete with Saint Trent and the holy Wingate/Holloway kids. They didn't like me and urged her to move out once the business started having trouble," Keith said. "I've reached out to her, but she's made it clear she doesn't need me anymore."

"She might need you, Uncle. They think it was an inside job."

"Do they?" Keith asked. "That would make sense. Only someone with access to the login information of someone at the top of the corporate structure would have been able to set that up."

Brian leaned back, taking another sip of his drink. "Do you have any idea who that could be?"

"I have an idea," Keith said. "You wouldn't believe me if I told you."

"Who do you suspect?" Brian asked, leaning forward, but his uncle had turned his attention to the basketball game playing on the big screen. Keith mumbled something under his breath and Brian leaned in close to catch it.

He shook his head, unsure he'd heard the muttered comments correctly. But it had sounded like something that Brian hoped like hell wasn't true.

"Did you say *you* did it?" Brian asked, horrified.

"What, boy?" Keith murmured.

Brian stood up and walked over to his uncle. "Who do you think is responsible?"

"Given how Ava recently treated me, I suspect it was someone who was close to the family and got cut out because of small-minded assholes," Keith said.

Brian stared at his uncle. Was Keith saying he'd done it? The only person who was outside the family and had the kind of control that Keith mentioned was…*Keith*.

His uncle finished his drink and Brian made his excuses and left, getting into his car and sitting there for a long time. He'd probably heard that all wrong.

Maybe he'd wanted to hear Keith say something so that Brian would have a reason to go back to Piper, seem like he was the hero.

Yeah, that was it.

He drove home, but the next morning he couldn't keep from remembering what his uncle had said. After all, Keith had been on the inside for a while. It could have been anyone close to the family.

Suddenly Piper's reservations about his uncle made more sense. Had she picked up on something from Keith that the rest of them had missed?

Brian made up his mind to go to the investigator and mention that Keith thought it could be someone who'd been close to the family. Zeke had mentioned they were working with the FBI to track down leads.

Should he go to them? Could he trust the ravings of a drunk?

At best, his uncle would be investigated and cleared…

Brian's conscience wouldn't allow him not to report this. He knew what he needed to do. Piper had said her family was the most important thing to her, and loving her as he did, he wanted to help them in any way he could. Even if that meant turning in his own uncle.

Ava went to meet with her children about the investigation into Wingate Enterprises, and while she was gone Piper started baking pies for Thanksgiving. She wasn't a traditional person by nature but there was something about this time of year that always made her want to have pie. Her mother had started baking them on the first of November when Piper had been a girl.

Piper started with pecan—her favorite—and there was something soothing and homey about the scents that filled the kitchen in Ava's rented house. She baked pumpkin pie and apple and mincemeat. Then she moved on to breads—banana and pumpkin—doing everything she could to keep her mind off Brian. It had only been a few days since she'd ended things for good, but it felt like a lifetime since she'd seen him. And the more time that passed the harder it was to say to herself that they would ever make it work.

She was seeing all the obstacles again. They had always been there, but when she had been with Brian—really been with him, not in Royal where she fell back into childhood patterns and attitudes—those hurdles hadn't seemed as big or insurmountable. It was only when she was lying alone in her big bed, missing him, that she reminded herself she'd kicked him out.

She'd broken up with him and he'd probably come to his breaking—she quickly shut that thought down. It was pointless to start feeling sorry for herself. Those thoughts and feelings inevitably followed a breakup. She knew her flaws better than anyone and loneliness just made them stand out.

The front door opened, and she heard voices as Ava, followed by her children, entered the house. "Everything smells delicious in here."

"Thanks. I wanted to do something productive," Piper murmured.

"I'm not waiting for Thanksgiving to partake," Zeke said. "Unless…"

"Of course we don't have to wait. I'm ready for a slice of pecan pie," Piper said. "How'd the meeting go?"

"Well, better than I think we expected. Seems Brian was over at Keith's the other night and he said some leading…" Ava broke off and turned away.

"What did he say?"

"Brian said it might have been the alcohol, so we don't want to get too excited that this will lead to anything, but he mentioned that the embezzling and drug trafficking had to be an inside deal and that it had to be someone close to one of us at the top." She sighed. "That pretty much only leaves Keith. When Brian pressed him, he didn't say it out loud but winked and said he couldn't say more."

Brian? Why had Brian done that? Was he trying to prove he wasn't like his uncle? Of course, he couldn't. "That's good, but how are they going to use it?"

"They've asked him to wear a wire and go back

and see if Keith says anything else. Right now, it's all hearsay, which Brian was adamant wouldn't stand up in court," Ava said. "So he's going to try to see if he can get Keith to admit it again. Ironically it was breaking up with you that led to the conversation."

"Sorry about that, Piper," Harley said, coming over and giving her a hug.

"If it helps the family then it will be worth it," Piper said. They sat around the dining room table in the rented house drinking coffee and eating the pies she'd baked, and Piper realized something about home. With her sister and her nieces, nephews and their partners this *was* home. It wasn't the big Wingate mansion or her home in Frisco. It was these people and… Brian. She missed him at this gathering. He'd have loved it.

She had said some things to him that were going to be very difficult to retract because she had meant it when she said that family was the most important thing to her, but she had just realized that somewhere along the way Brian had become family to her, as well.

She wanted to text him but had no idea if he was with Keith or if she'd interfere with his sting operation so she kept her hands off her phone. Instead, she played canasta with some of her family, and smiled and pretended that she wasn't worried about Brian. Keith might not be a physical danger to Brian, but he was dangerous.

If he was to blame for everything, then he had a powerful hate for their family, and anyone who helped him would be branded a traitor, especially his nephew. She couldn't keep her mind from wandering to a worrying place, and she tried to force her thoughts to the present, but after everyone had gone home and she and Ava were alone, it was exponentially harder.

"I misjudged Brian," Piper said to her sister as they were sitting alone in the living room. "I'm surprised he's done this for us."

"I'm not," Ava said. "I saw his face when you ran upstairs the other night. He looked like you'd pulled his heart from his chest and stomped on it. We misjudged him. I'm sorry for my part in that."

Piper nodded. But there was a huge lump in her throat, and she couldn't speak. So she just curled up in the chair, her mind swirling with the thought that she might have been too good at letting her fears rule her mind, and as a consequence, had hurt Brian in a way that he would never forgive.

He might be helping out the Wingates just to prove to her she was wrong and then…he'd walk away leaving her with the knowledge that she'd lost the only man she should have trusted.

Piper stared into the fire, wishing she could go back but knowing she would have made the same choices as before. Because the truth was, she hadn't changed until she'd hurt him. She hoped it wasn't too late after everything was over with the sting that Brian was running to frame Keith and save her family.

Twelve

Brian hadn't expected Piper to call. That was understandable, considering what was currently happening with their families. He was letting her have some space to think, but when the time was right, he was going back for her.

He loved her.

And he wasn't letting her walk out of his life. Not again.

However, right now he had to do something else that he knew was right no matter how much he hated it. He stood in one of the rooms at the Texas Cattleman's Club being wired by the local police. No one thought he should be seen leaving the police station, so they'd come to him instead.

He was going to try to get his uncle to talk and give up the name of the person he thought had committed the crime. That would make Keith an accessory because he hadn't come forward with the information voluntarily, but in the end, Brian had to believe it was the right thing to do.

Except that he wouldn't let his uncle get away with criminal activity. Obviously, it would be nice for Piper to see Brian as a hero, but morally it was wrong. So even if he hadn't been going out with her, he would have done this. Brian still wasn't one hundred percent sure what his uncle would say when he went back to talk to him since Brian couldn't ask leading questions. He had to just let the conversation make its way to Ava. *Let Keith take it there*, the agent who'd briefed him had said.

Brian was almost ready to go over to his uncle's house. His parents were expecting him back in Dallas for Thanksgiving, so if he didn't get the information today, he'd have to try again in a few weeks. The FBI agent and the Wingate family wanted the information sooner rather than later, and Brian didn't blame them at all.

He rubbed the back of his neck and put on his shirt over the wire.

"Okay, when you talk, the recording will start," the agent told him. "It's voice activated so you won't have to do anything. As a reminder, don't bait him. If you do that it will make it harder to use it in court. It might be enough to indict but we want a conviction too."

"Yeah, I got it. The other night he started talking about it when I brought up Ava's sister…" Brian paused. "I think he saw us as both loving the same type of woman."

"Just use your gut. You know him and you know the law. Don't feel like you have to force it, either," the agent said. "If you do that you won't sound like yourself."

Brian listened to more advice from the agent, and after he tested the device the agent left him alone. Brian sat there in the room at the back of the club going over the evening in his head. The other day, Keith had already been drinking. What if he wasn't today?

Then he took a few deep breaths and put on his lawyer persona. Sure of where he needed to be and what he wanted to have happen. He wasn't going to be more ready than this.

Leon and his friends were in the bar again and waved him over, but he pointed to his watch and made a *maybe next time* gesture before walking out. Dusk was falling and the November evening was crisp and cold. Starting to feel more like the holidays, he thought. He remembered the plans he'd made with Piper that would probably not be happening now.

Brian exhaled roughly. He didn't kid himself into thinking that bringing information to help clear her sister and family was going to make it any easier to win Piper back over. She needed to get to the point where she could trust him to stay. And trust herself enough to admit she loved him.

Piper usually had a pretty clear read on most people. He wondered what it was she'd seen in him that had led her to that conclusion, but then he shook his head and pushed all of that aside.

The only way he was going to get Keith talking about Ava again, regardless of whether he'd been drinking or not, was to convince his uncle that he hated Piper Holloway and the Wingate family as much as Keith must.

He went off book and stopped at the liquor store and bought a couple of bottles of Jack Daniels. He'd never drive drunk so he drove to the park near Keith's house and had a few swallows to give his breath the smell of the liquor and then spilled a little on his sleeve so it would seem like he'd been drinking all day.

To be honest, he might have been doing that if Keith hadn't said what he had the other night. Brian would have gone home and drowned his heartache in whiskey. Somehow doing this was almost cathartic.

He felt like at least Piper would be able to see he was a good, decent man. Maybe it would be enough to make her see that he'd never meant to hurt her the way he had. After driving the short distance to his uncle's house, he parked his car in the drive. He had poured out three quarters of one of the bottles and was holding it loosely in one hand, and he had a full bottle in the other hand.

Brian knocked on the door and waited. The housekeeper showed him to Keith's den where he was drinking, and when his uncle looked up and saw him, he welcomed him in.

"Glad you're back, son. No man should have to deal with a broken heart on his own," Keith said.

"I agree, Uncle," Brian replied. "I brought a bottle for you."

"Come in and we'll get started on it," Keith said with a grin.

Brian took a deep breath and stepped into the den, not knowing what his uncle was going to say. But he needed to get to the bottom of this. And then he'd figure out how to win Piper back.

He'd made a promise to himself that he wasn't going to let her walk out of his life again.

And he'd meant it.

"It has been a crazy year," Brian said.

As an opening gambit he wasn't sure it was a great one, but he needed to lead the conversation naturally to Ava and the sabotage at Wingate Enterprises. And frankly, at this time of year, he always reflected on the past.

"Opening your own law firm is quite an accomplishment. I know your daddy is proud of you, as he should be," Uncle Keith murmured.

"He is," Brian said. "He and Mama are anxious for me to settle down."

"Be careful who you choose, boy," Keith said. "I know you said you were dating Piper. Are you sure that's over?"

"Probably. My parents thought she seemed great, and they were not happy that we broke up. They don't get it like you do…" He knew he was laying it on a bit thick, but he needed to establish a rapport with his uncle. Make them the same. In one way they were. Piper had dumped him because she thought he wanted to change her. Which was beyond ridiculous. But honestly, he wished she'd seen that he wanted her just the way she was.

"Those Holloway women can singe a man to his core," Brian grumbled. "Even Trent didn't always have it smooth with Ava. He used to tell me about her stubbornness."

"God save me from that hardheadedness. Piper is so sure she sees me better than I see her," Brian said, knowing he had to be bitter and angry if he wanted Keith to start spilling. "Like she knows me at all."

"Ave never really saw me either. Just saw what she needed to in me," Keith told him. "I was there when Trent was sick and she started leaning on me to help out at the office. Just lend a hand because she was overwhelmed."

"You did a good thing," Brian said. The way his uncle was talking today, Brian felt more confident that Keith would give up the name of the insider who'd betrayed the family, and he was already determined to represent Keith if any charges were filed against him. Right now, he just sounded like a man who'd lost the woman he loved.

"I did, didn't I?" Keith asked, taking another sip of his drink. "Of course, she didn't see that. As soon as we got back from Europe she started acting different."

"There was the lawsuit after a fire at their jet plant in East Texas," Brian pointed out. "I think that shook her."

"I get that, but I was her rock. I had her back," Keith said. "She should have leaned on me. I think it was Beth who started her thinking of me in a different way."

"How do you figure?"

"I could tell. I don't think the kids were comfortable with her spending so much time with me so soon after Trent's death. I could tell by the way she talked to me. Always a bit standoffish," Keith said.

"It had to be hard. I don't know what I'd do if Dad died and my mom started turning to someone else. Beth was probably just trying to protect her mom."

"Maybe."

"I'm sure that was it," Brian said.

"After that, all the inroads I thought I'd made with

Ava when we were abroad seemed for naught. Maybe I'm good enough for her to lean on during grief but that's it," Keith said bitterly.

"Grief is really funny," Brian said.

"Yeah. I thought that Ava was the love of my life," Keith said. "But as it turns out, she just took what she needed and gave nothing in return." Keith was getting angrier with each word.

"Like I was letting her stay at my house while hers was seized just because we were friends. She knew there was more between us."

Brian realized that they were starting into the kind of conversation that he needed Keith to have. He knew that anger was what would make Keith give up the guilty party. As hard as it was, he needed to put himself in Keith's shoes and imagine that he'd never be with Piper again.

"Piper is the same way. I gave her my heart. I told her I wanted her to be my everything and she threw it back in my face. I'm too young for her...girl, you should be so lucky to have man like me in your bed."

"You don't have to tell me, son. She always was a little too good for everyone else. Ava at least is a beauty, so it makes sense. But then, with Ava, she makes sure that everyone in the room knows she's it."

Ava did like the spotlight. Brian took another sip of his drink. He wasn't sure he could keep saying all this stuff about Piper. But so far, other than bitching about Beth, Keith hadn't even mentioned Wingate Enterprises. "She's a tough broad."

"She is. But even she can't control everything. The company that Trent built is in a freefall and she should have turned to me to help her. But she had to leave my house because of those children and nephews of hers. Zeke never liked me either."

"I wonder why?"

"They think I was controlling her. If I'd had that ability, she would be in love with me," Keith groused.

"She's not?" Brian asked. This was slipping out of his fingers; he could feel it. He needed to talk about wanting to get back at Piper. That was the only way he was going to get Keith to confess to anything, and if he didn't…well then, his uncle was a jerk but not a criminal.

"How much have you had to drink?" Keith asked. "She's definitely not."

"Like Piper," Brian said. "I wish there was some way to get back at her. To make her see that she shouldn't have rejected me."

"I'd go after her business," Keith replied. "Take everything else she has in her life and bring it to ruins. Let her see what it feels like to be ripped to shreds, then she'll have nowhere to turn but you."

"I don't think that would work…" Brian began. Definitely not liking the sound of this. What was Keith saying?

"You're right," his uncle said, taking another long drink. "Trust me. She'd have to lose everything..."

"Ava's lost everything, or at least had it threatened. You mentioned you know who it is. Should you go after them? Then you'd be her hero," Brian told his uncle, realizing as he said it out loud that he was doing just that. Trying to solve a situation that he wasn't involved in so that Piper would see him as her hero.

"Yeah, kid, it's not going to happen. I started with the fire and embezzling funds, hoping that would drive Ava into my arms, and then I planted the drugs, and everything was seized and she had no place to live. But even being under my roof wasn't enough. She's still lost to me. Because she's still in love with *him*. She'll never be mine."

Brian just stared at his uncle. He hadn't expected the confession he'd just heard. And seeing his uncle's anger, and understanding the heartbreak that had driven him, didn't help at all.

Ava was in a full-on bitchy mood, and then sorry for her bitchiness, but the atmosphere had been tense once the rest of the family had gone home. Ava was dealing with the fact that the man she'd trusted might have been working against her the entire time. Piper understood that her sister would have felt bad even if she were the only one aware of it, but now everyone knew about Keith's betrayal. And that kind of weakness had always been her sister's Achilles heel.

"When are they going to call?" Ava asked for the fifteenth time.

"Whenever they have something. You and I might think it should be over with quickly, but I can't imagine getting Keith to confess something is going to go quickly," Piper said. She was riding a high thinking about Brian doing this for them and she acknowledged, since they still hadn't talked, that she had no clue if he was doing it for her. But deep down she hoped he was.

"What are you smiling about?" Ava asked.

"Just thinking about Brian. I can't believe he is doing this for us," Piper admitted.

"Of course, he is. Everyone likes our family," Ava said. "Did you think he was doing this for you?"

Piper shook her head. She was willing to give her sister some leeway, given that she was on tenterhooks waiting to hear back from the investigator. Knowing that if it was Keith, Ava was going to have to work hard to get her kids to forgive her and to forgive herself for not seeing that her friend was capable of this. She was lashing out, but Ava had always known just how to say the thing that hurt the most. And Piper wasn't going to take it anymore.

Maybe it was that she'd lost Brian because of her fears, and he was standing up doing the decent thing no matter what she'd said to him. Maybe it was her inner wise goddess finding her backbone now that she'd decided to fight for her man. Or maybe she'd just had enough after a lifetime of her older sister bullying her whenever Ava was feeling vulnerable. But something snapped.

"Brian is the kind of man you wish Keith had been. So whatever you are trying to say about him, save it! There isn't anyone to assign the blame to for this, Ava, except yourself." Piper released a quavering breath, trying to get her emotions under control. "Look, you were grieving and I can cut you some slack on that front. You were lost after Trent died and everyone gets that. But you made a mistake… and you're going to have to own it."

"And how do you propose I do that?" Ava huffed.

"Apologize to everyone and try to rebuild your relationships with them. But insulting me and being the queen bee isn't the way unless you want to spend the rest of your life alone." Piper narrowed her eyes at Ava. "There's no excuse for being unkind to me or your kids. This situation is difficult enough without that."

Ava stared at her, visibly taken aback, and Piper nodded at her sister. "And just so you know, if Brian will have me back, I'm going to spend the rest of my life with him. I don't care if you think he's with me for some ulterior motive or if you don't approve. It's my life and I live it on my own terms."

As soon as she heard those words, Piper realized

that her past fears had been dictating her behavior since the night of the gala. She'd fallen back into those old patterns as if Brian was her ex-fiancé. As if Brian wasn't the only man she'd fallen in love with after a lifetime of being good on her own. She didn't *need* a man in her life, but she *wanted* Brian. And Ava better get on board with that.

"Oh, and one more piece of advice? Call your kids."

"And what should I say?" Ava asked wearily.

"Tell them you love them and that you screwed up. It won't be an easy conversation, but taking responsibility will go a long way in mending fences. Now I'm going up to my room to sketch," Piper said, turning to leave the living room, but Ava stopped her, touching her arm as she walked by.

Her sister stood up and hugged her tightly. "I'm sorry, Pip. I didn't mean any of that. I just am so scared. I hate to think that everything Trent and I built over a lifetime has been destroyed by a man who we thought of as a friend. And you're right—I am to blame but admitting I screwed up this big… it scares me."

"It scares everyone," Piper said, hugging her sister and then stepping back. "But if everyone knows it was you and you don't acknowledge it, then it will fester and grow. And losing the business is one thing. It can be rebuilt. Losing the family…even the almighty Ava Wingate couldn't handle that."

Her sister wiped away her tears and nodded. "I couldn't. I'd be nothing without my family. I wish I'd been better about protecting them."

Protecting them. Piper had been trying to protect Brian from her own fears and she'd hurt him to do it. But she knew that she couldn't and wouldn't do that anymore. "Everyone is an adult, Ava, they don't need you to protect them that way. They need you to treat them as equals and respect them."

Ava nodded. "How did you get to be so smart?"

"My big sister is a good example," Piper said.

"I love you, Pip," Ava murmured.

"I love you too."

Thirteen

Brian left his uncle's house just after midnight. He was pretty sure they had enough on the tape to indict Keith but he wanted to make sure. He would go back again if he needed to. His uncle had been crazed with anger and bitterness but also that sad love tonight and since Brian hadn't been drunk there had been no denying that Keith was behind all of the criminal activity.

He had to pull over once he was out of his uncle's neighborhood. God, he couldn't believe the lengths Keith had been willing to go to in order to keep Ava in his life. To make her love him.

That kind of manipulation made him sick. Brian

hated everything he'd heard tonight. And all the things he'd had to say. He knew that he'd needed to, in order to get the conversation going, but he'd never expected his uncle to confess to everything.

Brian wondered if there was some kind of mental illness in the man. Though he knew from personal experience that losing a woman he loved could cut deep.

He drove to the police station while calling Miles Wingate.

"This is Miles."

His voice was rusty with sleep and Brian realized he might have waited until the morning, but since Miles had been on this from the beginning, he knew the other man would want to know what had happened that evening. He took a deep breath.

"Miles, it's Brian. Sorry to call so late but I've just left my uncle's house and he admitted to everything. He wanted to ruin your mother and your family. He blames y'all for her not loving him, but he really hates her for pushing him aside. I am headed to the police department so the lead investigator can take the wire off, but I wanted to give you a heads-up."

"Thanks, man. I can't believe he admitted it," Miles said. "Do you think it's enough to arrest him?"

"I do," Brian said. "But I'm not a criminal lawyer so it's just what I know from school not from practice. But I'm pretty sure the DA will be able to get a warrant for his arrest soon. With what you've uncovered and his confession they should be able to put together the pieces."

"Damn. I knew it was him in my gut, but I never thought we'd get him like this. Thanks again, Brian. Good night."

"Good night," Brian said.

He hung up, wanting to call Piper but at the same time wanting to finish his part in the investigation. Also, once she heard what he'd said on the tape would she believe anything else he said? And the issue between them was still Piper's belief that he wanted children more than he wanted her. He rubbed the back of his neck as he went into the police station and saw the lead investigator waiting for him.

"I've been listening in. Dude, you were good. I filled in the assistant district attorney, as well, and he's taking the transcript to a judge to get a warrant for Keith's arrest. He should be back soon. Normally we wouldn't do this in the middle of the night, but as slippery as Keith has been everyone wants him in custody. He might realize what he told you and try to leave Royal or even the country."

"He was almost passed-out drunk when I left, but I'd try to get there first thing in the morning before he can remember what he said. I…are you going to share the recording with the Wingate family?" Brian asked.

"Yes. I think they'll want to hear it," the lead investigator said.

"Would you…ask them to think kindly of me? I had to say some of those things to get him talking…"

"I'm sure they will understand," the detective said.

But Brian wasn't so sure. And he knew that Piper would be hurt by the things he'd said. He should text her, but he was done with middle-of-the night-calls. So he went to his home in Royal after he left the police station and found himself online looking at the digital image of the portrait that Piper had made of him. How could a woman who saw straight to his soul not have known he loved her?

He knew he'd never said the words, that admitting to loving someone like Piper frightened him. She was so self-contained. So sure and confident, he knew she didn't need a man even though he wanted nothing more than to claim her. To find a way to make sure she was his…

Regardless of how the two of them worked out he was happy for his part in helping to catch Keith. He almost texted his dad because he knew his father would want to know what his brother had been up to, but he knew better than to do anything until Keith had been arrested.

He didn't want to taint the arrest or give Keith's attorneys any ammunition to use to get him off the charges. And Keith had good lawyers, so Brian was sure it was going to be an uphill battle in court.

He closed the laptop and tried to go to sleep,

but honestly, he couldn't. All he could think about was Piper. Something Keith had said kept running through his mind, about not being able to make her love him. He would never try any of Keith's tactics to get Piper to love him, but he did realize that if she didn't love him maybe she'd said what she had about children to let him down easy. Maybe she hadn't loved him from the beginning, and if that was indeed what was at play here, then it might be time for him to move on.

Or, at the very least, go back to Dallas, away from Royal and Piper and the entire Wingate family.

Piper woke to the news that Keith had been arrested. Her entire family was gathered in the kitchen of Ava's rented house. Her sister was more animated than she'd been since Piper had come back to Royal. She saw relief on her sister's face, now that they had Keith's confession.

Beth and Harley stood close to their mom and Piper couldn't help but think that the worst was probably over now. "What happened? Did Brian get a confession?"

"He did," Harley said. "Piper, he was great. He didn't mention Mom at all…just let Keith bring it around to her."

"I knew he was responsible but hearing the hate in his voice. I had no idea that he'd become so bitter," Beth said.

"You heard the tape?"

"It's a digital recording," Ava told her. "You don't want to listen to it, Pip. Brian had some things to say about you… I don't think he meant them, but it's nothing you want to hear."

Piper wondered what Brian had said. Ava was correct in that she didn't need to hear it. She knew what she wanted from the future and anything that Brian had said in order to get Keith to confess was alright with her.

"Where is he?" she asked. She wanted to go to Brian and thank him for what he'd done for their family. Piper would use it as an olive branch to get a conversation going, then…then she was going to take a big risk and just tell him how she felt. Be the woman he'd awoken with his passion.

"Keith?"

She'd been thinking about Brian, but she did want to know where Keith was, as well. Plus she wanted to talk to Brian about how she felt before she let anyone else know—even her family. "Yes."

"He's being interrogated at the police station. They brought him in for questioning and then arrested him. I think they'll be a bail hearing soon," Beth said. "That's what I heard from the lead investigator. This is such a relief."

"It really is. The boys are heading over and I think we are going to issue some kind of statement," Ava added.

Piper hugged her sister and her nieces before leaving them to talk Wingate business. She pulled her phone out of her pocket just to make sure she hadn't missed a text or call from Brian, but she hadn't.

Piper: Thanks for helping my family. Can we talk?

Brian: I'm at the diner if you want to come and join me for breakfast.

Piper: Give me thirty minutes and I can be there.

Brian: Sounds good.

She had wanted a more private place for their talk but didn't blame him for suggesting the diner. He had been through a lot when he'd come to visit her the last time. She got dressed, fixed her hair and was out of the house in ten minutes. Faster than she'd gotten ready in a long time. But she missed Brian and she was fed up with the distance between them.

Piper knew they had a future. She'd made up her mind when she learned what he'd done for her family. Also she was tired of hiding from life and only pouring her passion into her art. She wanted to live in color with Brian. They brought out the best in each other, and more than anything, she wanted him in her life.

She parked near the diner in Royal and several townspeople stopped her to tell her how glad they were that an arrest had been made, and though some others might have believed the gossip about her family, they never had. Piper had to bite her lip to keep from smiling or saying something sassy as the sentiment was repeated several times. Ava was going to love this reversal of fortune.

Brian was seated in a booth near the back and she made her way over to him. Several people tried to stop her, but she just smiled and waved off their apologies. Royal had been quick to turn on her family, but she knew that was because of the strong sense of justice in the town. They were going to be all over Keith now.

She slid into the booth across from Brian and he smiled when he saw her. He looked tired but was truly a sight for sore eyes.

"Thank you," she said.

"It was nothing."

"It *wasn't* nothing," she insisted. "What you did for my family…especially after how I treated you—"

"It's okay, Piper," he said. "I'm just glad I could help. Turns out your breaking up with me was just the thing to push Uncle Keith into confessing his plot. So maybe I have you to thank."

She shook her head, reaching over to put her hand on top of his. "No. I wish I could have handled things better. You have never been anything other than a gentleman and I shouldn't have gone off like that."

Brian turned his hand in hers and rubbed his thumb over her palm before drawing back. He didn't want to touch her, she thought. *That's not good.*

This wasn't going to end the way she wanted it to, and she had no one to blame but herself.

"No, you shouldn't have," he said. "But I do understand why you did. I think I was moving too fast, afraid to lose you, and then I did anyway. But we hadn't been together long enough to have the conversation you needed to have, and I am sorry for that."

"Me too," she admitted. She noticed the waitress standing a short distance away waiting for her to look up.

The waitress hurried over, poured Piper a cup of coffee and took her order before leaving the two of them alone again.

"Listen, did you hear the recording of Keith's confession?" he asked.

"No. Ava said I didn't need to. She said you had done what you had to in order to get him talking."

Brian swallowed and nodded. "She is right. I had to convince him that I hated you, Piper, and the only way I could do that was by saying some things that could never be true. You are hardheaded but I love that. So strong and independent, and to me that's what makes you who you are. To Uncle Keith, those are the very things he hated about Ava. He wanted her to depend on him, to need him and only him."

"You're not that kind of man. You want to stand next to your woman not make her stay in the shadows."

"I do."

He leaned across the table and kissed her. Piper heard a smattering of applause around the diner, and as their lips parted, she realized that there were some things that were better done in private. This conversation was one of them.

"What do you say we go back to my place and talk details?"

"Naked details?" she asked coyly.

"Anything the lady wants," he said. She scooted out of the booth and he followed her, throwing some bills on the table to cover their food and then leading Piper out of the diner. As soon as they were in the parking lot and out of sight, he pulled her back into his arms.

Fourteen

Piper hadn't thought she could be this happy with anyone after her engagement had been broken but Brian was making her rethink so many things. His house in Royal was a large, sprawling two-story modern ranch. It was quiet as they entered, and he carried her up the stairs to his bedroom.

She knew if they were going to have a future together, she owed it to him to explain her past. She wanted him to understand why she just didn't think she could bring herself to try something as permanent as marriage again.

He put her on her feet on the thickly carpeted floor.

"Um, come and sit down next to me on the bed," she suggested. "It will make it easier to tell you if we're not standing."

He toed off his shoes, climbed into the center of his king-sized bed and beckoned her to come sit next to him. She had to smile at him. Her heart was full of joy and she had to wonder if she was holding to this one old fear for a foolish reason.

But she remembered how it felt to be engaged and then to suddenly be unengaged. She would much rather be Piper and Brian than have any other pressure.

"I was engaged… I think I mentioned it when we were at the gala," she said.

"You did."

"Things were going well and I thought we'd be married soon, but the doctor noticed something abnormal in my yearly pap smear so he called me back in and that's when he told me that it would be very difficult for me to have children," she said, remembering her confusion when he'd said it. "I have a lot of polyps in my uterus. Anyway, none of that matters. I told Ron—my fiancé—what the doctor had said and he asked *how* difficult it would be. I said I hadn't asked but Ron was insistent. So I went back for another appointment and the doctor said that I had a less than four percent chance of conceiving."

She sat down on the bed, staring at Brian's kind eyes and sexy face, and realized how hard this was to talk about. She'd never had to tell anyone the next part. Not even Ava. But she wanted Brian to know. Needed him to understand she hadn't been overreacting when she'd broken up with him. And knowing he cared for her made it easier for her to confide in him.

"Ron was waiting for me when I got home. I told him what the doctor had said and he got very angry and said that was it. We couldn't be married because the entire point was to have a family…" Piper's voice cracked. "I said that was fine. We could just be a couple. He rejected that and told me he wanted more from life than a would-be artist partner and no kids. So I gave him back his ring…well, sort of threw it at him…and told him to kiss my ass."

"You should have done more than that. What a bastard," Brian said. "But his shortsightedness is my gain. You know I don't care about anything but you."

"I do," she whispered. "When everything happened with Ron I promised myself I'd never be that vulnerable again. I channeled all of my passion into my art, and that worked until you came along." She met his eyes. "I hope you know I feel the same about you, but I don't want to be engaged."

"Fine by me. We aren't living it the dark ages," he said with a wink. "As long as I'm yours and you're mine, I'm okay."

"Same here," she said.

Brian leaned forward and pulled her into his arms, drawing her back against his chest. He rested his head on her shoulder and one big hand cupped her breast while the other spanned her waist, the heat of his body warming hers.

They fit perfectly together, something she'd always thought was an urban legend. But there was nothing fake about Brian Cooper. He'd gone above and beyond to prove himself to her and she couldn't believe she'd found a man she could trust with her battered heart and wounded soul.

A partner for the wise goddess she'd become, and she wasn't about to let him go now.

He rolled her over on the bed, coming over her, resting his arms on either side of her body.

"I am so glad you came up to me at the reception," she murmured.

"Me too. I'd been crushing on you for the longest time and I knew I had to make a move, or I'd regret it for the rest of my life."

"You would have," she said, wiggling her eyebrows at him. "You would have missed my kisses."

He brought his lips to hers. "You mean like this?"

His mouth was firm and he took his time kissing her, rubbing his lips back and forth until her mouth parted and she felt the humid warmth of his exhalation in her mouth. He tasted so…delicious, she thought. She wanted more and opened her mouth to invite him closer.

She thrust her tongue into his mouth and rubbed it over his teeth and then his tongue. He closed his teeth carefully over her tongue and sucked on her. She shivered in delight.

His taste was addicting, like the taste of Baileys on a cold fall night. Yes, she thought, she wanted much more of him, not just his kisses.

She put her hands on his shoulders and then higher to that thick black hair and pushed her fingers into it. Brian Cooper was hers now.

His hands moved over her shoulders, his fingers tracing a delicate pattern over the globes of her breasts. He moved them back and forth over the swells until the very tip of his finger dipped beneath the material of her top and reached lower, brushing the edge of her nipple.

Exquisite shivers racked her body as his hands continued to move slowly over her. He pushed her sweater up and over her head, tossing it to the floor next to the bed. She wore a lacy camisole and he leaned back to look down at her chest.

"I would have missed seeing you like this," he said. "I would have had to make do with my imagination."

"You would have," she murmured, arching her back and watching his eyes move down to her breasts. Her nipples were hard and pointed under the lace.

He wrapped his hands around her waist and drew her to him, lifting her. "Wrap your legs around me."

She did and immediately was surrounded by him.

His mouth was on her breasts, his hands on her butt, and he suckled her gently. Nibbling at her nipples through the fabric of her camisole as he massaged her backside. When he took her nipple into his mouth she felt everything inside of her tighten and her center grow moist.

His mouth…she couldn't even think. She could only feel the sensations that were washing over her as he continued to focus on her breasts.

One of his powerfully muscled thighs nudged her legs apart and then he was between them. She felt the ridge of his cock rubbing against her pleasure center and she shifted against him to increase the sensation.

She wanted to touch him, had to hold him to her as his mouth moved from her breast down her sternum to her belly button. He looked up at her and for a moment their eyes met. "I can't imagine my life without you, Piper."

He lowered his head again and nibbled at the skin of her midriff, his tongue tracing the indentation of her belly button, and it felt like each time he dipped his tongue into her that her clit tingled. She shifted her hips to rub against him and he answered her with a thrust of his own hips.

His mouth moved lower on her, his hands finding the waistband of her jeans and undoing the button, then slowly lowering the zipper. She felt the warmth of his breath on her lower belly and then the edge of his tongue as he traced the skin revealed by the opening.

The feel of his five o'clock shadow against her was soft and smooth. She thought she'd learned everything she needed to about Brian, but it seemed there was still more for her to experience.

"Lift your hips," he commanded.

She planted her feet on the bed to lift them up, and felt him draw her jeans over her hips and down her thighs. She was left wearing the tiny black thong she'd put on that morning.

He palmed her through the panties, and she squirmed on the bed. She wanted more.

He gave it to her, with his hand on her most intimate flesh and then with his mouth as he drew her underwear down by pulling with his teeth. His hands kept moving over her stomach and thighs until she was completely naked and bare underneath him. Then he leaned back on his knees and just stared down at her.

"You are so gorgeous, Piper," he said.

His voice was low and husky and made her blood flow heavier in her veins. Everything about this man seemed to make her hotter and hornier than she'd ever been before.

"It's you," she said in a raspy voice. "You are the one who is making me feel that way…"

"I'm nothing more than the only man for you," he said.

She shuddered at the impact of his words. He *was* the only man for her, and she knew it. She couldn't be happier to know she'd spend the rest of her life with him. Pleasure rippled through her as he lowered his head again and rubbed his chin over her mound. Just a back and forth motion that made her clit feel engorged. Then he tilted his head down until he could trace the line of hair from the Brazilian wax on her nether lips.

"This is the one thing I should have done when we made love at your place the first time."

"You did," she reminded him.

"I should never have left. Just kept us in bed so we could learn each other's secrets and know each other's heart."

He parted her with the thumb and forefinger of his left hand and she felt the air against her most intimate flesh and then the brush of his tongue. It was so soft and wet, and she squirmed, wanting— no needing—more from him.

He scraped his teeth over her and she almost came right then, but he lifted his head and smiled up her body at her. By this time, she knew her lover well enough to know that he liked to draw out the experience.

She gripped his shoulders as he teased her with his mouth and then tunneled her fingers through his hair, holding him closer to her as she lifted her hips.

He moaned against her and the sound tickled her clit and sent chills racing through her body.

His other hand traced the opening of her body. Those large, deft fingers made her squirm against him. Her breasts felt full and her nipples were tight as he pushed just the tip of his finger inside of her.

The first ripples of her orgasm started to pulse through her, but he pulled back, lifting his head and moving down her body. Nibbling at the flesh of her legs. She was aching for him. Needing more of what he had been giving her.

"Brian…"

"Yes?" he asked, lightly stroking her lower belly and then moving both hands to her breasts where he cupped the full globes.

"Take me now," she said. "It feels like a hundred years since I've had you inside me and I need you now."

Piper was shivering with the need to come and wanted more from him. She wanted his big body moving over hers. Wanted his cock inside of her, thrusting hard and deep. She reached between their bodies and stroked him through his pants. Impatiently, she lowered the tab of his zipper, but he caught her wrist and drew her hand up above her head.

"Don't do that or I'll lose it. I thought I'd never have you again," he said.

"Me either. That's why I need you. Now."

"Okay," he said, lowering his body over hers so the soft fabric of his shirt brushed her breasts and stomach before she felt the masculine hardness of his muscles underneath. Then his thigh was between her legs, moving slowly against her engorged flesh, and she wanted to scream as everything in her tightened just a little bit more.

It wasn't enough. She writhed against him, but he just slowed his touch so that the sensations were even more intense than before. He shifted again and she felt the warmth of his breath against her mound. She opened her eyes to look down at him and this time she knew she saw something different. But she couldn't process it because his mouth was on her.

Each sweep of his tongue against her clit drove her higher and higher as everything in her body tightened, waiting for the touch that would push her over the edge. She shifted her legs around his head, felt the brush of his silky-smooth hair against her inner thighs.

Felt his finger at the opening of her body once again and then the delicate biting of his teeth against her pleasure bud as he plunged that finger deep inside her. She screamed his name as his mouth moved over her. The first wave of orgasm rolled through her body.

Her hips jerked forward and her nipples tightened. Piper felt the moisture between her legs and his finger pushing hard against her G-spot. She was shivering and her entire body was convulsing, but he didn't lift his head. He kept suckling on her and driving her harder and harder until she came again, screaming with her orgasm as stars danced behind her eyelids.

She reached down to claw at his shoulders as pleasure engulfed her. It was more than she could process, and she had to close her eyes. She reached for Brian, needing some sort of comfort after that storm of pleasure.

He pulled her into his arms and rocked her back and forth. "I can finally breathe now that you are back in my arms."

"Me too."

Brian couldn't let things rest until he'd addressed what had been said on the recording. The things he'd said, well, he hadn't meant any of them. "In case you ever listen to the recording of myself and Keith, please know that I didn't mean a word—"

"Brian, I know that," she said, reaching up to touch his face as they lay nestled in each other's arms. "You were doing what you had to in order to help my family."

"I was. Honestly, I never expected any of what he confessed. I thought, at best, that he might have known the real person who had mucked things up… not that he was the mastermind behind all of it. But he wanted to burn down everything Ava loved."

Piper shook her head. "I read an article a few years ago about how fine the line between love and hate is, but to be honest I never believed it until now. I am so sorry you had to do that."

"I'm not. When you told me everything, I realized that despite telling you I was mature and feeling in my heart that I was ready to make a life with you, I'd never really given us a chance to talk. I just rushed you to bed and then wanted to make it permanent," he said.

She smiled at him. "Don't take all the credit for rushing me to bed."

He was starting to think that Piper wasn't just here to thank him for helping to catch the criminal responsible for the trouble at Wingate Enterprises. She was talking to him in a careful way. She'd explained how her past affected her feelings about marriage and…did she regret ending things with him?

He took a deep breath, not sure if his heart would survive her rejecting him again. But he had to at least try one more time. He knew his life was going to always seem a little too gray and routine without Piper in it. Stretching one arm along her back, he looked into those beautiful eyes of hers. God, how he'd missed her. It might have only been two days since he'd last seen her but, in his heart, it felt much longer.

A lifetime had passed since he left her at Ava's house. So much had happened and changed, but the one thing that hadn't was how he felt about her. He wanted her as much now as he ever had. If not more so. Having confronted his uncle and heard the way the other man had tried to ruin Ava's life, and by extension, Piper's, had made him want to right the wrongs done to them.

And he had.

There was nothing left but to bare his soul to Piper and see if she'd have him back in her life. If she'd give him the second chance that he so desperately wanted. And if she said no? God, it would hurt like hell, but he'd respect her decision.

"You know I did all that for you," he said. "I mean, I couldn't let him walk away once he'd hinted that he might have had something to do with it, but I did it because you told me how much your family meant to you and I know deep in my heart that one day I want to be a part of your family. I want you to be my family—"

"Brian, I can't—"

He stopped her words with his fingers over her lips.

"Piper, marriage doesn't matter. I want you by my side. I love you," he said. "I know that I probably am moving too fast, but time isn't going to change how I feel about you and I don't want to have to pretend that it will."

He put his hand on her naked hip and waited to see what she would say. She leaned up, meeting his gaze with her own. "I can't have kids. That's not going to change. It might matter to you, Brian, when everyone else is starting a family and you are stuck with—"

"The most gorgeous woman in Texas? The only woman I've ever loved? Unless you don't love me, Piper, there is no reason for us not to be together. There are plenty of kids in the world who need a family, and when we are ready, they will find us."

She smiled at him and he realized he was holding his breath. She hadn't said she loved him or that she wanted him back in her life, but he'd laid it all bare. It was up to her to make the next move, and whatever she decided, he'd abide by it.

Even if it killed him.

"I love you, Brian. If you're sure—"

"Dammit, Piper, I'm a man of my word."

"You are," she admitted, wrapping her arms around his shoulders as she kissed him. It seemed to him that she might never let go; hell, he wasn't going to let go for a long time either.

"I wish I'd taken the time to see what you were hiding from me," he said. "I'm so sorry you were hurt."

"You couldn't have seen it, Brian. I was hiding it even from myself. I thought I had everything I needed until you came along and danced with me at the wedding reception, and suddenly I was thinking how nice it might be to have you in my life."

"Forever."

"Forever."

Epilogue

Hosting Thanksgiving at her house wasn't something Piper had anticipated doing, but she wanted to have her family around Brian and herself. She was little nervous, which was silly because it wasn't as if she needed her family's approval to be with the man she loved, but she still wanted it. And Brian had decided to forgo his traditional attendance at the Cowboys game since he said there was nowhere he'd rather be than by her side.

The turkey was in the oven and Brian was in the big living room, acting as the host. He had the Macy's Thanksgiving Day parade on because that was one of her nonnegotiables. Brian had brought his mom's famous cinnamon pumpkin bread and his parents were coming by later. The arrest of Keith hadn't been easy for the Cooper family, but they weren't that close to his uncle so it wasn't as bad as it could have been.

Beth and Camden arrived first. She sent Camden into the living room with Brian who had a drinks station set up in the corner at a large antique bar she'd purchased a few years ago in an estate sale. Next were Harley, Grant and Daniel, and then Zeke and Reagan, and Luke, who she knew was feeling stressed about finding new ways to revive Wingate's businesses. Finally, Sutton and his fiancée, Lauren, arrived with Ava. Sebastian had texted he would be there in time for football and turkey, and Gracie had gone to Florida to spend the holiday with her family. Piper had everyone together.

She had an open-plan kitchen that spilled into the living room, so everyone moved back and forth between both rooms. Ava pulled her aside and Piper was wary about what her sister would say. Ava had thought Brian was too young for her.

"I was wrong about Brian," Ava said. "Let's get that out of the way first. He's a great man and perfect for you. And I will never be able to forget what he did for us."

She hugged her sister. "Me either. I can't believe how happy I am."

"I'm glad. It's about time you found someone to share your life with," Ava said.

Piper couldn't agree more, and when it was time to sit down to the main meal, she reached under the table to squeeze Brian's hand as she invited everyone to go around and say what they were grateful for.

Much of the sentiment was for new loves, their cleared family name and their plans for relaunching Wingate Enterprises now that Keith was in jail. Ava was happy to have her family around her. And Piper thought she saw in her sister's eyes that she wouldn't ever take them for granted again.

"I'm glad Keith is in jail, but rebuilding is going to take a lot of time," Sebastian said.

"Y'all are up to the challenge," Piper murmured.

"We are."

"Are y'all making it official?" Zeke asked Brian after they'd had dessert. "Just asking to make sure you're taking proper care of my auntie."

Zeke winked at Piper.

"We are official, though we're not really concerned with things like marriage. But y'all can get used to seeing me with Piper for the rest of our lives."

Zeke toasted them and everyone joined in. Piper realized how blessed and thankful she was for her family.

* * * * *

Don't miss a single installment in
Texas Cattleman's Club: Rags to Riches!

Available June 2020 through January 2021!

The Price of Passion
by USA TODAY *bestselling author Maureen Child*

Black Sheep Heir
by USA TODAY *bestselling author Yvonne Lindsay*

The Paternity Pact *by Cat Schield*

Trust Fund Fiancé
by USA TODAY *bestselling author Naima Simone*

Billionaire Behind the Mask *by Andrea Laurence*

In Bed with His Rival
by USA TODAY *bestselling author Katherine Garbera*

Tempted by the Boss
by USA TODAY *bestselling author Jules Bennett*

One Night in Texas
by USA TODAY *bestselling author Charlene Sands*

WE HOPE YOU ENJOYED
THIS BOOK FROM

HARLEQUIN
DESIRE

Luxury, scandal, desire—welcome to
the lives of the American elite.

Be transported to the worlds of oil barons, family dynasties,
moguls and celebrities. Get ready for juicy plot twists,
delicious sensuality and intriguing scandal.

6 NEW BOOKS AVAILABLE EVERY MONTH!

*Looking to settle down, Alaskan CEO Garth Outlaw
thinks he wants a convenient bride. What he doesn't
know is that his pilot, Regan Fairchild, wants* him. *Now,
with two accidental weeks together in paradise, will the
wife he needs be closer than he realized?*

Read on for a sneak peek at
The Wife He Needs
by New York Times *bestselling author Brenda Jackson.*

"May I go on record to make something clear, Regan?" Garth
asked, kicking off his shoes.

She swallowed. He was standing, all six feet and three inches
of him, at the foot of the bed, staring at her with the same intensity
that she felt. She wasn't sure what he had to say, but she definitely
wanted to hear it.

"Yes," she said in an almost whisper.

"You don't need me to make you feel sexy, desired and wanted.
You are those things already. What I intend to do is to make you feel
needed," he said, stepping away from the bed to pull his T-shirt over
his head and toss it on a nearby chair. "If you only knew the depth
of my need for you."

She wondered if being needed also meant she was indispensable,
essential, vital, crucial…all those things she wanted to become to
him.

"Now I have you just where I want you, Regan. In my bed."

And whether he knew it or not, she had him just where she
wanted him, too. Standing in front of her and stripping, for starters.
As she watched, his hands went to the front of his jeans.

"And I have you doing what I've always fantasized about, Garth.
Taking your clothes off in front of me so I can see you naked."

She could tell from the look on his face that her words surprised
him. "You used to fantasize about me?"

"All the time. You always looked sexy in your business suits, but my imagination gets a little more risqué than that."

He shook his head. "I never knew."

"What? That I wanted you as much as you wanted me? I told you that in the kitchen earlier."

"I assumed that desire began since you've been here with me."

Boy, was he wrong. "No, it goes back further than that."

It was important that he knew everything. Not only that the desire was mutual but also that it hadn't just begun. If he understood that then it would be easier for her to build the kind of relationship they needed, regardless of whether he thought they needed it or not.

"I never knew," he said, looking a little confused. "You never said anything."

"I wasn't supposed to. You are my boss and I am a professional."

He nodded because she knew he couldn't refute that. "How long have you felt that way?"

There was no way she would tell him that she'd had a crush on him since she was sixteen, or that he was the reason she had returned to Fairbanks after her first year in college. She had heard he was back home from the military with a broken heart, and she'd been determined to fix it. Things didn't work out quite that way. He was deep in mourning for the woman he'd lost and had built a solid wall around himself, one that even his family hadn't been able to penetrate for a long while.

"The length of time doesn't matter, Garth. All you need to know is that the desire between us is mutual. Now, are you going to finish undressing or what?"

Don't miss what happens next in...
The Wife He Needs
by Brenda Jackson, the first book in her
Westmoreland Legacy: The Outlaws series!

Available November 2020 wherever
Harlequin Desire books and ebooks are sold.

Harlequin.com

HDEXP1120

Get 4 FREE REWARDS!

We'll send you 2 FREE Books <u>plus</u> 2 FREE Mystery Gifts.

Harlequin Desire® books transport you to the world of the American elite with juicy plot twists, delicious sensuality and intriguing scandal.

FREE
Value Over
$20